ZAPPED!

The lights came back on, and Callie stared at her clothes in disbelief. Her light jeans were smeared with dirt and stained with soda.

"We'd better take you home and get you cleaned up," Frank said.

Then Joe heard a shriek from the stage. What he saw made him forget all about Callie. Now that the crowd had fled, Joe had a clear view of the stage in front of Daffy Disc Music.

Where two performers had stood moments before, there was now only one.

The other—Ron Minkus—was sprawled on his back motionless, clutching his microphone in a strangely stiff grip. . . .

Books in THE HARDY BOYS CASEFILES™ Series

Available from ARCHWAY Paperbacks

THE HARDY BOYS

CASEFILES™

NO. 106

SHOCK JOCK

FRANKLIN W. DIXON

AN ARCHWAY PAPERBACK
Published by POCKET BOOKS
New York London Toronto Sydney Tokyo Singapore

AN ARCHWAY PAPERBACK *Original*

An Archway Paperback published by
POCKET BOOKS, a division of Simon & Schuster Inc.
1230 Avenue of the Americas, New York, NY 10020

Copyright © 1995 by Simon & Schuster Inc.
Produced by Mega-Books, Inc.

ISBN: 0-671-50429-0

First Archway Paperback printing December 1995

10 9 8 7 6 5 4 3 2

THE HARDY BOYS, AN ARCHWAY PAPERBACK and colophon are registered trademarks of Simon & Schuster Inc.

THE HARDY BOYS CASEFILES is a trademark of Simon & Schuster Inc.

Cover photograph from "The Hardy Boys" series © 1995 Nelvana Limited/Marathon Productions S.A. All Rights Reserved.

Printed in the U.S.A.

IL 6+

Chapter

1

"Now, *THIS* IS THE PERFECT GIFT for my mom," said Chet Morton, his round face lighting up as he ran a finger over a high-tech waffle iron in the appliance section of Martin & Company Department Store at the Bayport Mall.

Behind him, his friend Joe Hardy chuckled and said, "Hey, big guy, don't you mean that's the perfect gift for *you?*"

Chet spun around to challenge Joe, but as he moved, his expression changed to a sheepish grin. "I guess you're right," Chet admitted. "Back to square one."

With Christmas less than a week away, the Bayport Mall was packed with shoppers. It was obvious to Joe that all the stores were making a giant effort to be festive. There were red and green and sparkling decorations everywhere. The department store sound system was piping in carols, and all the salespeople were wearing elf hats reading Santa's Helper. Between the busy staff and the frenzied customers, though, the scene reminded Joe more of a demolition derby than a holiday shopping scene.

Glancing around, Joe noticed that his brother, Frank, had linked arms with his girlfriend, Callie Shaw, so they wouldn't be separated in the flood of people.

As they approached him, Joe pointed out a gleaming silver-and-black appliance on the counter beside his older brother. "I've got a great idea, Frank," he said. "Why don't we get Mom and Dad a microwave?"

"Why? So you can make popcorn whenever you want?" Frank said, and shook his head.

Callie neatly sidestepped a woman who was making a beeline for the waffle irons. "I'm not getting my folks anything that involves work, and you guys shouldn't, either," she scolded. "I'm getting my mom something pretty and frilly. Let's go to ladies' lingerie on the third floor."

Panic crossed the faces of all three boys.

"Isn't it time for lunch?" Frank muttered, checking his watch.

"I'm starving," Chet said.

"I vote for lunch, too," Joe said. "Majority rules."

Callie slowly shook her blond head and followed her three male companions out of the store. Chet took the lead, cutting a straight path through the shoppers to a vacant table in the bustling food court.

"Chet," Frank said, "if you could do that on a football field, you'd be an all-star."

"I probably could if they had free hot dogs and pizza waiting behind the goalpost," Chet said.

Callie saved the table while the boys filled their trays with hot dogs, burgers, and fries. When they came back, she went over to the Veggie-teria stand and returned with a small green salad and a bottle of mineral water.

"What's with the bunny food, Callie?" Chet said, eyeing Callie's plate with mild disgust. "Are you on a diet or something?"

She raised an eyebrow. "Choosing not to clog my arteries with fat and oil has nothing to do with my weight. I'm just treating my body with the respect it deserves."

"Oh," Joe said with a wicked grin. "I thought it might have something to do with the three pairs of jeans you couldn't get into—according to Frank."

Callie turned bright red and gave Frank a look that would have burned a hole in an Abrams tank. Frank, in turn, shook his head at his brother. Joe quickly focused back on Chet, who was chowing down on his second of four hot dogs.

3

"Chet, I can almost hear your arteries screaming 'Help me! Help me!' "

Chet shrugged and picked up a few fries from his plate. "It's genetic," he replied. "Look at your dad, and then look at mine. I'm predestined to be big."

It was true. Fenton Hardy, a well-known private investigator, was tall and trim, and his sons took after him. Laura Hardy, the boys' mother, was attractively slim. The only Hardy who came close to Chet's body type was their aunt Gertrude—and she was older.

"Sure, part of it's genetic," Frank said, "but eating less and exercising always cuts some weight. That's a fact."

"Well, in any case, it's too late to start my diet today," Chet said, standing up to clear his tray. "Let's get back to shopping."

The others followed Chet's lead and returned to their search for perfect holiday gifts. At the north end of the mall they could see a huge crowd gathering in front of Daffy Disc Music.

"What's going on?" Callie asked, holding on to Frank's shoulder for balance and craning her neck to see.

Joe stood on his toes and caught a glimpse of someone facing the crowd. He could see a thatch of dark hair, but the speaker's face was obscured. Something about the man's head was familiar, though, but Joe couldn't place him.

Then all at once he recognized the voice booming from the loudspeakers. "Hey, that's Ron Minkus!" he exclaimed.

The foursome quickly found a spot to view the small stage that was set up in front of the music store. Ron Minkus, obnoxious radio personality and major celebrity, was apparently broadcasting live from the mall with his sidekick, Marian Brown. Joe knew that Minkus had a reputation as an "equal opportunity offender." He made fun of all people—even the handicapped were targets. Whatever anyone held dear, Minkus made a joke about it. His show boasted a following in the hundreds of thousands, and it seemed that many of his fans had turned up at the mall that day.

"Let's go," Callie said. "I hate this guy."

"Just a minute," Joe said, obviously curious about what Minkus had in store for suburban Bayport. Neither brother liked the radio show, but Frank also was curious to see what the trash-talking DJ was up to.

Ron Minkus pointed to a nasty-looking bunch of young hoods with shaved heads. "Hey, what's with you guys?" he shouted. "Did you shampoo with your sisters' hair remover by mistake?" The crowd laughed as the thugs glowered. The biggest of the bunch yelled an angry threat back at Minkus, who cheerily replied, "I'm *real* scared, cue ball. Why don't you come up here and let us know what you're thinking—if anything?"

The big hood, egged on by his friends, elbowed

his way through the crowd to join Minkus on-stage.

"I challenge you to a battle of wits, my friend," Minkus said. "If you win, I'll give you a thousand bucks. If I win, you take all your knuckleheaded friends and go home to your mommies. Deal?"

The big guy shrugged and nodded.

"How do you keep a moron in suspense?" the DJ asked.

A mixture of puzzlement and concentration crossed the gang leader's face. Minkus started counting down.

"Five, four, three, two, one—you're outta here." The DJ jerked a thumb toward the doors.

"So what's the answer, Minkus?" the bulky hoodlum yelled.

"I'll tell you tomorrow," Minkus crowed.

The crowd laughed and cheered.

"Huh?" By now the big guy was really confused.

"That's the answer, fathead. 'How do you keep a moron in suspense'—'I'll tell you tomorrow!' " Minkus egged on the crowd to cheer more. The big guy shook his fist at the DJ, vowing revenge, as his friends dragged him off.

Joe watched intently as the hoods slinked off toward the food court. Minkus had already turned his attention to a group of girls holding signs that read Women Against Minkus. Clad in tie-dyed T-shirts and ripped jeans, the girls were chanting, "Minkus hates women! Minkus hates girls!"

"Aaah, you chicks don't know what you're talking about," Minkus drawled. "I love women. Why, I even own one or two. Why don't you shave your legs and put on some nice dresses so you can look pretty?"

At this insult a howl replaced the group's chanting.

"So much for a peaceful demonstration," Joe said as one of the girls hurled a tomato in Minkus's direction.

"We are *leaving*," Callie said from between clenched teeth. She grabbed Frank's arm and turned to go.

As they began making their way toward an exit, a collective gasp rose up from the crowd. The four friends whipped around and saw Minkus hand his redheaded sidekick a long aluminum pole. Dangling from a rope noose at the end of the pole was a stuffed Santa Claus doll. As Marian Brown held the pole out, Minkus moved a cigarette lighter closer and closer to the Santa doll, threatening to set it on fire.

"Wait a second, Callie," Frank said. "This could get ugly. He's ignoring every rule in the fire code."

Callie stopped and stood with her arms crossed, a frown creasing her pretty face.

"Christmas is a commercialized farce!" Minkus shouted. "Put down your credit cards. Stop spending money you don't have on gifts that your friends and relatives don't want anyway."

As Minkus spoke he brought the lighter closer and closer to the stuffed Santa's beard. "Santa is a lie—rearrange the letters and what do you get? SATAN. Santa is Satan!"

Minkus hollered like a TV preacher. While his supporters cheered, families with small children started to flee.

Sal Tarentino, the owner of Daffy Disc, was not pleased with the antishopping rant, either. Joe could see the short, balding man glaring out from the doorway of his record shop. I guess he figured sponsoring the popular DJ's appearance would boost sales, Joe thought. But everybody's watching, not shopping, and now Minkus was telling them *not* to shop.

Minkus turned up the lighter, holding the flame to the doll's gloved hand as Marian sputtered with laughter. The fabric burned briefly but quickly fizzled—apparently, the toy was not very flammable. Minkus tried lighting a foot with the same result.

Furious, the DJ broke open the plastic lighter and dumped all its fuel on the Santa doll. Then he turned to the crowd. "Anybody got a light?"

At least a dozen lighters clattered onto the stage.

Then Tarentino blew up. "Stop it, Minkus!" he yelled, arms waving. "You'll burn the whole place down." The crowd was too loud, so the DJ didn't hear the shopkeeper.

Minkus picked up one of the lighters and tried to set the doll on fire. Tarentino darted back into his store and seconds later reappeared dragging a large fire extinguisher. To the delight of the crowd, he started hosing down Minkus, Brown, and the Santa doll with thick white foam.

Minkus grabbed his microphone, ducking the stream of foam, and yelled above the noise, "Pay no attention to the man behind the fire extinguisher!"

As the DJ and his sidekick tried to shield their faces from the foam, Frank and Joe began to notice a buzzing noise. It seemed to come from Minkus's own speaker system and grew louder by the second.

The buzz from the speakers suddenly built into an angry crackling noise. Then came a very loud bang! The lights went out, and Joe thought he heard a lone scream before everything was drowned out by sounds of horror from the crowd.

People began screaming, alarms went off, and shoppers slammed into one another in a mad dash to get out of the mall. Joe heard someone yell, "Fire!"

Then he heard Callie crying for help as she was knocked to the ground in the general panic.

Joe, Frank, and Chet had to use all their football skills to save her. Joe and Chet formed a human shield to divert the stampede as Frank lifted Callie to her feet.

"Are you all right?" Frank asked as the four

fought their way to a raised alcove next to the Jeans Hut.

"I—I guess so," Callie stuttered.

The lights came back on, and Callie stared at her clothes in disbelief. Her light jeans were smeared with dirt and stained with soda.

"We'd better take you home and get you cleaned up," Frank said.

Then Joe heard a shriek from the stage. What he saw made him forget all about Callie. Now that the crowd had fled, Joe had a clear view of the stage in front of Daffy Disc Music. Where two performers had stood only moments before, there was now one. The other—Ron Minkus—was sprawled on his back motionless, clutching his microphone in a strangely stiff grip.

Chapter
2

A HUSH PASSED over the mall at the sight of the fallen DJ. Then, thinking it was just one of Minkus's famous pranks, the crowd's panic gave way to an amused murmur. "Hey, Minkus, quit lying down on the job!" someone shouted.

Minkus didn't move. Frank heard Chet mutter, "Come on—a joke's a joke. . . ."

Marian Brown knelt next to the prone DJ and put her hands on his shoulders. "Come on, Ron, wake up!" she said. Minkus's head lolled as she shook him.

Frank was concerned. "I don't think he's kidding around," he said.

The scattered laughter and catcalls from the crowd were drowned out by a sudden wail from Marian. Police responding to the earlier distur-

11

bance rushed onto the stage. Marian started crying as the officers pulled her away from Minkus. A stunned hush fell over the crowd as people realized this wasn't a performance.

"This *is* for real," Joe said as he, Chet, and Callie followed Frank to the front of the crowd. Bayport's finest were already cordoning off the stage.

A team of paramedics, on-site because of the Christmas crowds, carefully laid Minkus on a gurney and wheeled him through the crowd. Frank spotted Officer Con Riley, the Hardys' best contact on the force, trying to clear a path for the gurney.

"Is he going to be okay?" Frank asked the officer after Minkus was wheeled away.

"What happened, anyway?" Chet wanted to know, joining them.

"He's still alive," Riley answered. "Saving him will be up to the doctors.

"Move along, folks," Riley said in a louder voice. "There's nothing to see. The accident has been cleared."

"Are you sure it was an accident?" Joe piped up.

Riley studied the younger Hardy seriously. "We won't know anything for sure until we investigate," he said. "Right now, it looks like some sort of electrical malfunction." He glanced around at the crowd. "Although with this guy's enemies—who knows?"

"Do you think he's going to die?" asked Callie, who looked as though she was about to cry.

Frank put an arm around her and said, "I don't know, Callie. But let's get out of here. Suddenly I don't feel like Christmas shopping."

"I sure hope he's going to be okay," Chet muttered, his skin pale.

They trudged out to the Hardys' van in silence. As Joe started the engine, Frank glanced at the dashboard clock. "I completely forgot about the party," he said.

"How can you think of a party at a time like this?" Callie asked.

"Because we're going to be right in the middle of it as soon as we get home," Joe said glumly.

It was a Hardy family tradition to host an open house every year on the Saturday before Christmas. Mrs. Hardy and Aunt Gertrude had been preparing all week.

"I forgot, too," Callie said. "I even told your mom I'd help serve. How am I going to act cheerful after this?"

Frank gave her shoulder a little squeeze and said, "Mom will understand if you don't want to do it."

"That's okay," Callie replied. "My mom and dad are at my aunt's for the day, and I don't feel like being alone right now."

Joe glanced over at Chet, who sat next to him, staring straight ahead. "Chet, do you want to come to the party or should we drop you at home?"

"I think I'll just go home if it's okay with you guys," Chet said.

"We'd be glad to have you," Frank said. "There'll be lots of refreshments."

When Chet didn't answer, Frank touched his shoulder and said, "Are you sure you're okay?"

"I was just thinking about Ron Minkus," Chet said. "He may have acted like a jerk, but a lot of people get a kick out of his show."

"Are you one of those people?" Frank asked.

"I listen to Minkus occasionally," Chet admitted.

"You do?" Callie burst out.

Chet sounded defensive. "He could be really funny."

After dropping Chet off at home, Frank, Joe, and Callie drove to the Hardys'.

"Look at that!" Callie exclaimed as the house came into view.

White Christmas lights were draped over the bushes at the front of the house, and a large plastic Santa, lit from inside, was patrolling the roof with three of his reindeer. Snow was falling lightly, making the scene look just like that on a Christmas card.

"We haven't had the Santa up since we were little kids," Frank said. "Looks like Dad was busy this morning."

Joe chuckled and said, "I'm glad we missed that part of the tradition."

There were so many guests' cars on the street

and in the driveway that Joe had to let Callie and Frank out in front of the house while he drove off in search of a parking spot.

"Look at me." Callie sighed. "I'm a mess. Let's sneak in the back so no one sees me like this."

"You can borrow some of my mom's clothes," Frank said, leading the way to the kitchen door. No sooner had they opened the door than their path was blocked by their aunt Gertrude. She made clucking noises of dismay and said to Callie, "What happened to you, dear?" Then, without waiting for an answer, she hustled Callie upstairs. "I'm sure we can find something of Laura's to fit you. Would you like to take a shower?"

Frank smiled as his aunt, still chattering, led his girlfriend up the stairs. He was just about to sneak a canapé off a tray when his mother stepped into the kitchen.

"Frank Hardy, where have you been?" Laura Hardy demanded, worried.

"Mom, I told you we were going to the mall," he reminded her. "Something awful happened. We saw—"

"We have a house full of guests asking for you and your brother," she interrupted. "By the way, where's Joe? Vanessa called several times. She sounded upset."

"He's parking the van," Frank said. "Mom, you won't believe what happened—"

"I bet *I'll* believe it," a voice boomed from behind mother and son. Frank and Joe's father,

Fenton Hardy, was a tall, dignified man. That day, probably at the prodding of his wife, he wore a tie decorated with little elves that lent a festive air to his usual weekend outfit of khakis and buttondown shirt.

"Chief Collig was a guest here earlier and had to take an emergency call in the den," Fenton explained. "It seems Ron Minkus had some kind of accident at the mall."

"Who's Ron Minkus?" Laura asked her husband.

"Ron Minkus is what they call a 'shock jock' on the radio," Frank said. "You remember him. He led a group of animal rights activists who broke into the university last year and let the lab monkeys out of their cages."

"Oh, of course," she recalled. "He almost went to jail for that stunt."

"The chief said Minkus's situation wasn't good," Fenton said.

"What exactly *did* happen at the mall?" Laura Hardy asked. "And where's Callie?"

"Upstairs with Aunt Gertrude," Frank said. "Minkus got a bad electrical shock, and passed out, while all the lights in the mall went out. The crowd started stampeding and Callie got knocked down—" He raised a hand when he saw his mother's expression of concern. "She's okay, really. Just some dirt and soda on her clothes. Aunt Gertrude took her upstairs to raid your closet."

"What about your brother?" she asked. "Vanessa said she needs to talk to him."

The party was in full swing when Joe Hardy came in the back door. He would have preferred to come home to a quiet house, but knew this party meant a lot to his mom. He tried hard to get into the holiday spirit.

Laura Hardy gave her younger son a quick welcome kiss and said, "Call Vanessa. She phoned, sounding almost frantic."

Joe frowned. He'd met Vanessa Bender on a case involving her mother's computer animation business. Vanessa's good looks and cool head had attracted him, and they'd been dating ever since. If anything could make his computer-whiz girlfriend frantic, it must be serious.

"Don't worry, Mom, I'll call her right away," Joe said. "You go back to the party."

Joe dialed Vanessa's number several times, but it was busy. He hung up the kitchen phone, turned, and bumped into Callie, who had come into the kitchen in one of Laura Hardy's dresses.

"Hi, Callie," Joe said. "Have you seen Frank?"

"I was just looking for him," Callie answered.

Joe stepped into the dining room and scanned the party for Frank. His brother was talking to "Uncle Bill," a long-time friend of the family. Joe went over, said hello, and after a proper amount of time deftly excused himself and Frank.

"Thanks for the rescue," Frank said. "Every time Uncle Bill tells one of his Korean War stories, there are more and more soldiers on the other side—and it takes longer to tell.

"What's up with Vanessa?" Frank continued. "Mom says she's been calling."

"I know," Joe said, "but when I just tried to call her back, all I got was a busy signal. I'd like to go over there. Do you think Mom would be upset?"

"I'll cover for you. It'll be cool," Frank said.

"Well, I'm off, then," Joe said. "I'll be in touch."

It started snowing harder as Joe drove to the Benders' house, wondering what Vanessa had wanted. As he pulled up to the front of their old farmhouse, nothing looked amiss. Joe could see the glow of Vanessa's computer screen through her second-floor bedroom window. A Christmas tree shone through the first-floor window. Jumping out of the van, Joe ran through the thick snowflakes to the front door.

The door swung open before Joe could even knock. "Glad you could make it, Joe," Vanessa's mother said, ushering him in.

"Is Vanessa okay?" Joe asked.

"Physically, yes," Mrs. Bender said. "She's upstairs. Go on up."

Vanessa was red faced and teary eyed as she let Joe into her room. "I'm so happy to see you," she said, giving him a hug.

"What happened? Are you okay?" Joe said.

"I'm fine," Vanessa said. "It's my friend Sarah who needs your help. You have to meet her."

"Let's go. I have the van," Joe said.

Vanessa shook her head. "No, no . . . over here."

Joe was puzzled as his girlfriend walked over to her desk. There was no one else in the room.

"She's *here,*" Vanessa explained, pointing at her computer.

Joe became even more puzzled as Vanessa sat down at her desk. Then he noticed the lights on her computer modem were lit up bright green and red—just like the Christmas tree downstairs. "So *that's* why your phone was busy," he said.

"Huh? Oh, right." Vanessa shrugged. She motioned for Joe to pull up a chair. "Do you remember my telling you about my on-line friends?" she asked.

"Sure," he said.

"Well, Sarah is one of them. She needs your help. It's her father—" Vanessa glanced at Joe. "Her name is Sarah Minkus."

"As in *Ron* Minkus?" Joe said.

"His daughter," Vanessa said. "We've been communicating by computer for about three months now.

"Just a second," she said, and began typing into her computer. "Sarah, I'd like you to meet that friend I was telling you about—Joe Hardy. I think he can help you."

The words "Hello, Joe" appeared on the screen.

Vanessa slid the keyboard over to Joe and said, "Go ahead, introduce yourself."

"Hi, Sarah," Joe typed. "I was at the mall and saw your father's accident. Is he going to be all right?"

There was a long pause. Then a single line of glowing letters appeared across Vanessa's screen. Joe gasped as he read them aloud.

" 'My father is dead.' "

Chapter

3

JOE SAT BESIDE VANESSA and stared in shock at the computer monitor. Shortly, more words appeared: "We got the call from the hospital about half an hour ago. They"—again, there was a pause—"couldn't revive him. He may have been murdered."

"Would you take over and see if we can meet her in person?" Joe asked Vanessa.

After Vanessa got an okay from Sarah, Joe went downstairs to phone Frank.

"So, we're going to see Sarah Minkus," Joe finished up. "We'll pick you up on the way if you want to go."

As he hung up, Vanessa bounded down the stairs with a slip of paper in one hand. She went to the back of the house to explain to her mom

21

where they were going, grabbed her coat, and followed Joe out the door. As they drove, Joe filled Vanessa in on what had happened at the mall earlier.

"Looks like Frank decided not to come alone," Joe said to Vanessa as they pulled up at the Hardy house. Beside his brother stood Callie and a familiar bulky shape.

"How's it going, Chet?" Joe asked as his big friend climbed into the van.

"It was too quiet at home," Chet said, "so I decided to check out your party. When I heard where you were going and why, I asked Frank if I could tag along." Joe glanced at Frank. "Is Mom upset that we're all bailing out?"

"No, of course not," Frank said. "Not after she heard why." He handed Vanessa a foil-wrapped package. "She even sent a goodie bag from the party for Vanessa."

Normally the goodies would have disappeared immediately, but they remained untouched as Joe drove out of town.

"I didn't know Ron Minkus had kids," Chet said. "He never mentioned them on the air."

"Well, maybe you missed those shows," Frank said. "You said you just listened sometimes."

"I guess it's more like sometimes I *didn't* listen," Chet admitted. "His show is a real eye-opener in the morning. It's a lot better waking up to jokes than a buzzing alarm clock." He sighed and stared out the window. "Guess I'll have to get used to my alarm now."

They spent the rest of the ride in silence, except for Vanessa's street directions. They were heading down the coast to the nearby village of Clearpoint, which was considered a hideaway for the rich and famous. The Minkus residence was no exception. It had a gray stone wall with a high entrance arch and gate. The driveway beyond the gate was at least the length of a football field with a huge front lawn spreading out on either side of the drive. The house, a sprawling contemporary in stone and cedar, easily qualified as a mansion.

"Wow," Joe said.

But he wasn't talking about the size of the house. He was reacting to the horde of reporters and TV camera crews churning the snowy front lawn to slush.

"What are we going to do?" Vanessa asked. "She'll never be able to come out to us through this mob."

"I've got an idea." Joe handed Vanessa the cellular phone as he pulled away from the entrance arch. "Call Sarah and tell her to go out the back and meet us one block over."

"Great," Vanessa said.

Joe pulled the van around the corner. It was a long drive to the next street because the houses in Clearpoint were built on such big lots. They parked directly behind the Minkus estate in front of what appeared to be a miniature castle.

"Look at that place," Callie said. "It must have cost millions."

Just then a small figure appeared from behind the castle and cut across a field of virgin snow. Vanessa eagerly leaned forward and said, "That must be Sarah!"

"I thought she was your friend," Frank said. "Why don't you know what she looks like?"

"We've never met in person," Vanessa said. "Sarah, over here!" Vanessa hopped out of the van, ran over to the smaller girl, and embraced her. "Let's get you out of the cold."

Chet opened the back door and helped the girls in. Joe noticed that Chet was reacting clumsily—and then he saw why.

Sarah Minkus was a very pretty girl. Her eyes might be bloodshot from crying, but they were still large and green. She was slim, like a model from a fashion magazine. Her hair was long, curly, and brown, and her complexion was the color of Chet Morton's favorite drink—cocoa. Joe gave his brother a quick wink as Vanessa made introductions and Chet bustled to offer Sarah his seat.

Sarah clutched Vanessa's hand and said, "Thank you so much for coming. It means a lot to me."

"Come on, Sarah," Vanessa said, "it's the least I could do."

"We were at the mall today and saw what happened to your father," Frank said gently. "We're all so sorry."

Joe and Callie nodded.

"It must be awful," Chet said.

"And it keeps getting worse." Sarah huddled in her seat. "First the police came to the house to tell us about the accident. Then before Mom could even leave to go to the hospital, we got the call that Dad was dead. They were calling it accidental electrocution." Her green eyes welled up with tears. "Then, a little while later, we had a knock on the door. It was police detectives from Bayport. It turns out somebody tampered with Dad's microphone, so they're saying he might have been murdered. They're searching our house for clues right now."

Sarah put her face in her hands and leaned forward to rest her arms on her knees. Vanessa put an arm around her friend and said, "Maybe you've had enough for one day, Sarah."

"I'm okay," Sarah insisted, lifting her head. "It's just that—well, Mom hasn't really come to grips with any of this, and my sister is too little to understand what's going on. That leaves me to deal with Dad's—murder."

"I think that's where Frank and Joe can help you," Vanessa said.

"We'll do our best," Joe said. "Sarah, can you tell us about your dad?"

25

"Had he been acting any differently lately—nervous, threatened?" Frank asked.

Sarah thought for a minute. "My dad was a health nut," she said. "He was a vegetarian, took vitamins, jogged. We used to joke that he'd outlive us all. But for the past week or two, he'd been sick a lot."

"Your dad was a *vegetarian?*" Chet said.

At this Sarah had to smile. "I know," she said, "he always made fun of nature types on the air. But he was really different off the air—*really.*"

"How do you mean sick?" Frank asked.

"He was tired a lot," Sarah told him. "And he was having trouble keeping food down. Mostly he complained of stomach cramps."

"Did he go to the doctor?" Callie asked.

Sarah nodded and said, "The doctor told him he was under too much stress and he should take a vacation. But of course Dad couldn't or wouldn't. He loved to be home for the holidays. It was his favorite time of the year."

"What?" Joe, Frank, Callie, and Chet all exclaimed in unison. They'd seen Minkus's Christmas "spirit" on display at the mall that afternoon.

"Dad would dress up like Santa every year," Sarah said. "He went to housing projects to give out gifts to poor kids. He never talked about it to the press."

"I thought he was cool," Chet said. "I just didn't know *how* cool."

"He was the greatest," Sarah said proudly. She pointed at her right hand. "You probably figured out from the color of my skin that the Minkuses aren't my birth parents. Before we were adopted, my baby sister, Tori, and I were stuck with foster parents who only kept us for the money the state gave them. They'd skimp on our food, and sometimes I had to shoplift formula or baby cereal for Tori."

"What happened to your birth parents?" Chet asked.

"Something went wrong when Tori was born, and our mother died. My dad couldn't handle being a single parent, and they didn't have any family."

"That's horrible," Callie said. "How old were you?"

"That was five years ago. I was eleven. Tori was about a year old," Sarah said. "She's lucky she can't remember how it was in the foster home."

"How did you end up with the Minkuses?" Joe asked.

"Well, my mom—Judy Minkus—was a social worker," Sarah revealed. "When she and my dad decided to have a family, they thought it was kind of selfish to have kids when there were already so many needy children. My mom used her contacts to find us. Judy and Ron Minkus are the kindest, gentlest people you could ever meet." Sarah stopped to wipe her tears.

"No offense," Joe said, "but you'd never guess from listening to 'The Ron Minkus Show.' He seemed like such a—"

"Joe, have you ever heard of acting?" Vanessa snapped. "Do you think Arnold Schwarzenegger goes around shooting people and blowing up buildings after work?"

"Sorry, Sarah," Frank spoke up. "My brother has this bad habit of running his mouth before his brain cuts in."

"No, I'm the one who's sorry," Sarah said. "You don't even know me and you're offering to help. I know how most people felt about my dad. That's because they only saw one side of him. A couple of years ago, even my mom had to stop listening to 'Radio Ron.' That's what she called his on-air personality. It bothered me to listen to his show, too."

"We know your dad liked to tick people off," Frank said, getting back to business. "But was there anyone in particular who might want to hurt him?"

"Maybe your father had a fight with someone," Joe suggested. "Or maybe there were threatening phone calls, or letters—"

"There was one thing," Sarah said. "A few months ago—it must have been during the summer, because I wasn't in school—I got the mail and there was a sheet of paper stuffed inside the mailbox. It read, 'Minkus = Death.' "

"Did you show it to the police?" Joe asked.

"I didn't even show my parents," Sarah admitted. "I threw it out."

"You just tossed it?" Joe asked.

"I know, I know, that was stupid of me," Sarah berated herself. "I didn't want my dad to be upset by it."

"Yes, but—" Joe said. Then before he could continue, Chet leaped to Sarah's defense.

Glaring at Joe, he said, "We're talking about something that happened months ago. Who could have guessed this might happen?"

Joe was ready to answer but never got the chance. As Chet finished speaking, there was the sound of tires screeching outside. Car doors slammed, and almost instantly there was a thunderous banging on the side of the van.

"You're surrounded!" a nervous voice blared over a bullhorn. "We're coming in! Do not move."

The van suddenly rocked, and the rear doors were flung open. Joe stared at four figures in black silhouetted against the snow. Each of them stood in a classic combat crouch, aiming an automatic pistol inside the van. They moved forward quickly, arms outstretched, weapons leveled, ready to fire.

Chapter
4

"POLICE! FREEZE! Put down any weapons and put your hands in the air!" The amplified voice was deafening in the close quarters of the van. "Come out with your hands up—now!"

Frank and the others shuffled out, hands raised. The police officers backed off, still covering them with their guns.

"Officer, is there a problem?" Frank asked. "We were just out here talking."

"Just talking?" said the officer in charge, who had put down his bullhorn. "You're parked out here in the middle of a snowstorm and you say you're *just talking?* Who are you? Are you going to tell us what you're up to or do we have to search your vehicle?"

Frank stepped forward, right into the firing

line. "I'm Frank Hardy, and this is my brother, Joe," he said. "If it's okay, I'll pull out my wallet and show you some ID."

"Take it slow," said the officer in charge. Frank gingerly reached for his back pocket. The officer checked Frank's driver's license, then waved for his fellow officers to holster their pistols. The rest of the teens followed Frank's example and showed some identification.

"You're Sarah Minkus?" the officer said, glancing from the photo on her ID card to her face. "Are these people holding you against your will?"

Sarah shook her head, wiping a tear from one eye.

"She just lost her father," Chet said. "We came to offer our help, but there was such a circus outside her house . . ."

The police officer nodded and said, "When we first got the complaints about your being parked here—"

Frank opened his mouth to speak, but the officer raised his hand. "One homeowner thought you were burglars, casing the neighborhood. We figured you were a news van, covering the Minkus case. Then we got a report that you had lured a member of the family out of the house, so we had to check it out as a possible kidnapping."

Vanessa's face was pink from the chilly air, but it got even pinker. "We didn't lure anybody," she said. "Sarah knew we were coming. I just suggested meeting her here to avoid being mobbed by reporters."

"Well, young lady, it worked a little too well," the officer said. "Next time do your talking over the phone." He turned back to Frank. "Frank and Joe Hardy, huh? Any relation to Fenton Hardy over in Bayport?"

"We're his sons," Frank said.

"I hear you guys have helped the force over there a couple of times," the man said. "Are you planning on getting involved in this case?"

Frank glanced at his brother, but the officer waved away an answer. "Never mind," he said. "The Bayport P.D. has jurisdiction. All we're doing is crowd control." He looked disgusted as he ordered his fellow officers back to their squad cars. "Do us and the neighbors here a favor—visit indoors, okay?"

The teens watched as the men got into their cars and drove off.

"If this is what happens when you park on the street in this town," Chet said, "what do they do if they catch you littering?" He took Sarah by the arm and began leading her back to the van, but she stopped.

"I'd better get home," Sarah murmured. "My mom will be worried."

"Are you going to be all right?" Vanessa asked. "Would you like me to sleep over?"

Sarah nodded gratefully. As Vanessa checked with her mom on the car phone, Frank and Joe did their best to reassure the girl that her father's killer would be caught.

"We've worked with the Bayport police a lot," Frank said, "and they're as good a bunch of cops as you'll find anywhere."

"And they don't waste time and energy arresting teenagers in parked vans," Joe grumbled.

"You guys will still help out, won't you?" Sarah asked.

"Count on it, Sarah," Chet said before Frank or Joe had a chance to answer.

"I'll give you guys a call tomorrow morning and make plans to meet," Vanessa added.

Frank and the others waved goodbye as the two girls trudged back through the snow toward Sarah's house.

"Sarah sure is cute," Chet said.

Callie began stamping her feet and rubbing her arms. "Right now I'm more concerned with all these cute snowflakes," she said, turning to Frank with a shiver. "This day has wiped me out. Would you mind dropping me at home?"

"No problem," Frank said. "How about you, Chet? Ready to go home?"

Chet didn't respond. He was still staring at the spot that Sarah and Vanessa had left, not even noticing the snowflakes melting on his face.

"Hello. Earth to Chet," Frank said, poking his friend in the arm.

Chet jumped. "What?"

"We're going to drop you off at home, okay, Chet?"

"Are you two going home?" Chet asked.

33

"Not right away," Frank replied. "I bet Con Riley's putting in some overtime on this case. Joe and I are going down to the station to try to get some information out of him."

"I'm going with you," Chet said.

Frank noticed the stubborn set to his friend's jaw. He shrugged and said, "Suit yourself."

They dropped Callie off at her house. When she went to kiss Frank good night, she whispered, "Chet is behaving very oddly."

"Tell me about it," Frank said.

When the Hardys arrived at the Bayport Police Headquarters, they found Officer Riley burning the midnight oil. He was examining photos of the microphone Ron Minkus had been holding at the mall that day.

"Whoever did this did it right," the officer revealed. "The electric jolt through the mike was enough to send somebody into the stratosphere." He pointed at the photo. "It was rigged to go off either when he flipped the Off switch or with a time-delay switch. They're taking it apart down at the lab right now."

Chet leaned forward, his eyes focusing on the picture of the mike. "Any leads?" Chet asked.

Frank shot his friend a warning look. Con Riley was friendly to the Hardys, but he was first and foremost a police officer. He might discuss a case, but he wasn't about to give away leads.

Riley put the photo facedown. "We know

somebody didn't like Ron Minkus," he said, "and whoever it was used this microphone to get rid of him. But that's about all we know—at least until after the autopsy." The police officer stroked the stubble on his chin. "Look, guys, it's late. But I'd like to ask you a few questions."

"Shoot," Frank said.

"I hear Minkus had a run-in with some thugs with shaved heads. Did you see it?" the officer asked.

"I saw it," Chet almost shouted. "They were standing by the Tijuana Taco stand. Minkus got one of them up on the stage and made a fool of him. Why? Do you think they had something to do with his murder?"

"Never mind," Riley answered, giving Frank and Joe a frown as if to say, "What's gotten into your friend?"

"We talked with one of Minkus's daughters," Frank told the officer.

"She's really nice—not at all what you'd expect," Chet interrupted.

"Settle down, Chet," Frank said. "I want to tell Con what Sarah found. It was a threatening letter—in the mailbox a couple of months ago."

"Interesting," the officer said, scribbling in his notebook. "I'm going to interview the family tomorrow. We had officers over there earlier, going through Minkus's office."

"Are you going to bring in those skinheads for questioning?" Chet asked anxiously.

"It's an option," Riley said, "but I don't know if it'd be justified at this point in the investigation." Riley gave all three teens a hard look. "I hope you're not planning to make this one of your junior sleuth projects. Anything you know, you should be telling me right now or as soon as you find out. And that's it. No interfering with our investigation."

"Is there anything else?" Chet asked. "Other evidence, maybe something from the crime scene?"

In spite of his gruff exterior Office Riley was a good guy at heart. But the day's events—and Chet's prying—were beginning to test his patience.

"I shouldn't tell you this," Riley said with a sigh, "but we did find something else at the mall. There was a homemade bomb under the stage. Lucky for us, it was badly made and it didn't blow up. Now, if you fellas don't mind, I need to get back to work. . . ."

Frank thanked Con, then led the way out. He waited until they were outside before he turned to Chet. "What's the big idea?" Frank demanded. "Why were you badgering Con Riley like that?"

"He was holding out on us," Chet replied.

"Of *course* he was holding out on us," Joe chimed in. "That's his job."

"He didn't have to tell us a single thing, Chet," Frank explained. "He was just being nice because he knew we had an interest in the case. We have to be careful because pushing him like that might lose us an ally."

"We wouldn't have found out about the bomb if I hadn't bugged him," Chet said as Frank got behind the wheel of the van and began navigating the icy roads home.

"Chet," Joe began, "your rabid interest in this case wouldn't have anything to do with a certain green-eyed girl we just met, would it?"

"Knock it off, Joe," Chet said. He paused, staring at his feet, then mumbled, "I know who those skinheads were."

"Who are they?" Frank asked.

"They call themselves the Bootstompers." Chet looked up, his face grim. "They're a gang of thugs—high school dropouts, mostly. I've seen them scare old ladies into giving them change in front of the arcade."

"That doesn't make them murder suspects, though," Joe said.

"Oh, no?" Chet asked. "Then why were they the first ones your friend Officer Riley asked about? You haven't seen these scum in action. Remember that demonstration for world peace last year? The Bootstompers charged in and ripped signs out of people's hands. They tried to drown out their songs with racist hate chants. It almost turned into a riot."

"I remember reading about that," Frank said. "Weren't several of those guys arrested for assault?"

Chet nodded. "They beat up a few people coming home from the rally. But the charges were dropped because the victims were afraid to testify. What does that tell you about the Bootstompers?"

"Chet, you seem to know an awful lot about these guys," Frank finally said. "Why didn't you tell Riley?"

"I have my reasons," Chet replied.

Frank didn't like the sound of this. Pulling the van to the side of the road, Frank shut off the engine and turned around to face his friend. "What reasons?" he demanded.

"There's only one way to beat them—by joining them," Chet declared. "Tomorrow I'm becoming a Bootstomper."

Chapter

5

JOE'S EYES WIDENED and he stared at Chet in disbelief. "What are you talking about?" he said.

"It's called going undercover," Chet said almost smugly. "As far as I'm concerned, those creeps are prime suspects in the murder of Sarah's father, and I'm going to catch them. It's the only chance any of us, especially the police, have of getting close to them."

"Undercover work can be very dangerous," Joe warned. "And it may be for nothing. Ron Minkus ticked off a lot of people. We have to consider everyone a suspect. What makes you put the Bootstompers at the top of the list?"

"You saw the way he goaded them at the mall," Chet said. "That was just a sample of what he's done to them. The Bootstompers are pro-gun, pro-war, pro-hate, perfect targets for Minkus. He had Bobby Hadrava, the head Bootstomper, on his show a few months ago and made a total fool of him."

"That probably wasn't too difficult," Frank said.

"Right, all he had to do was get Hadrava to open his mouth," Chet said. "By the time Minkus was done, Hadrava looked like a real moron. They got into a big argument, and Hadrava ended up throwing a chair at Minkus. Ron had to go to the hospital for fifteen stitches."

"This is the guy you want to get close to and spy on?" Joe asked.

Chet nodded. "Minkus pressed charges after the chair throwing, and Hadrava spent time in jail. I think that makes for a good motive—and I intend to find some solid evidence to back it up."

"Chet, he's no angel," Joe said. "But being an idiot with a bad temper doesn't make him a murderer."

"Why don't you let us go undercover with you?" Frank said.

"No way," Chet said. "It'll be hard enough getting them to trust one stranger—let alone three."

"You're probably right," Frank agreed. "But at least let us work out a plan to back you up."

"Okay," Chet said. "That sounds sensible. Here's where I get off. See you guys in the morning."

After dropping Chet at home, the Hardys drove straight home for a good night's sleep.

The next morning a fresh blanket of snow covered Bayport. There were perfect Christmas-card scenes everywhere, with colored lights brightening the gray skies and kids cross-country skiing down the unshoveled sidewalks.

"I keep forgetting we're only a couple days away from Christmas," Joe huffed as he and his brother shoveled their way to the van.

Heaving a load of snow over his shoulder, Frank said, "I know, and we still have Christmas shopping to do. Any bright ideas?"

Joe shook his head as he scraped snow off the windshield and said, "When you were downstairs, Vanessa called from Sarah's house. I said we'd stop by around ten."

"Well, while you were in the shower, Chet called," Frank said. "We're supposed to pick him up first."

"He's got a crush on Sarah, all right," Joe said.

"I can hardly wait to see how he tries to impress her," Frank said as he started the van.

When they pulled up to the Morton house minutes later, neither of the Hardys could believe their eyes.

"What did he do?" Joe said to Frank. Their friend stood waiting on his front porch, his head shaved bald. He was wearing a black leather jacket and motorcycle boots.

Joe couldn't help himself. He burst into laughter as Chet climbed in the side door of the van. "You look like a punk version of Curly from the Three Stooges."

"All you need is a giant number eight on the side of that dome," Frank said with a chuckle.

"I know I look like a jerk," Chet said, "but the Bootstompers would never trust me if I looked my usual handsome self."

Joe's expression grew serious. He had been hoping that, with a night to think it over, Chet would change his mind about going undercover. Instead, Chet seemed even more determined to carry out his plan.

After picking Callie up and explaining Chet's new look to her, they drove to the Minkus estate.

The front lawn was totally deserted as they pulled up the long drive to the front of the house. Vanessa and Sarah opened the door as soon as Joe rang the bell. Neither of them looked as if she'd slept a wink, but the girls weren't too tired to notice Chet.

Sarah's eyes widened with horror. "What did you do to yourself?" she asked an increasingly red-faced Chet.

"It's a disguise," Chet said. "I'm going undercover."

"We'll explain it all inside," Joe said. "We don't want our hairless spy to catch pneumonia standing out here, do we?"

Sarah looked a little confused but quickly led

her new friends to the den. In one corner a little girl who was a younger, smaller version of Sarah sat playing with a Malibu Mindy doll.

"Why doesn't that boy have any hair?" the little girl asked, staring at Chet.

"I'm not quite sure," Sarah said to her little sister. Tori Minkus invited Vanessa over to her dollhouse to play. Sarah turned to Chet and asked, "What do you mean by going undercover?"

Once Chet had explained his suspicions about the Bootstompers and his plan to infiltrate them, Sarah eyed him worriedly. "That sounds awfully dangerous," she said.

"I can handle myself, Sarah," he assured her. Joe noticed Chet was doing his best to suck in his stomach and puff out his chest as he spoke. "Frank, Joe, and I have taken on some nasty characters in our time, and we're all still here."

Callie stifled a giggle. Frank nudged her and whispered, "Let him be a tough guy. He wants to impress Sarah."

Frank forced out a cough and said, "Sarah, if you're feeling up to it, I've got a few questions for you."

Sarah seemed to remember all at once why they were there. She sat down on the sofa with her knees drawn up to her chest, her pain reflected on her face. "I keep forgetting he's dead," she said with a sigh. Callie plopped down next to her and rubbed her shoulders in sympathy.

"That note you found in the mailbox last summer—can you tell us anything else about it?" Frank asked. "What color was the paper? Did it come from a copier or a computer? Were there any other words on it besides the death threat?"

"I was racking my brain last night, trying to picture it," Sarah said. "I remember that the paper was shocking pink. And when I turned it over there was one word—a short one, like *bang* or *bam*. Something like that."

Joe snapped to attention. "Frank, remember that group of girls at the mall yesterday? Their signs said 'Women Against Minkus'—WAM."

"I've heard of WAM, I just never knew what it stood for," Vanessa called from across the room. "The kids in it seem harmless. Maybe a little dramatic. Last year they picketed the army-recruiting booth at the school career fair."

Callie spoke up. "Hey, if Chet can go under-cover, so can I. I'll join WAM and see what I can dig up."

"I doubt those girls could be behind a crime like this," Joe muttered.

"Ever hear of Lizzie Borden, genius?" Callie inquired. "Vanessa, when are you going to knock some sense into this guy?"

"He's hopeless," Vanessa said as she helped Sarah's little sister dress another doll, Malibu Mindy's friend L.A. Linda.

The sound of the doorbell interrupted their conversation. Sarah got up to answer it. She was even more troubled when she returned.

"What's up? More reporters?" Vanessa asked.

Sarah's brow furrowed. "No," she answered slowly. "It was the police. They wanted to talk to my mother."

"Maybe they caught the killer," Chet suggested.

Sarah joined Vanessa and Tori, obviously holding back tears. Callie turned to the Hardys and whispered, "What do you think this is all about?"

"We talked to Con Riley last night," Frank said. "He said he had to interview the family. It sounded routine."

A moment later Judy Minkus entered the room, and Joe began to suspect the interviews weren't going well. He could see Mrs. Minkus was an attractive forty-year-old brunette, but at that moment her face was streaked with tears. Con Riley and a Bayport detective the Hardys didn't recognize stood awkwardly in the doorway. Mrs. Minkus sat on the couch and motioned for her daughters to join her.

She stifled a sob as she said to her children, "I don't want you girls to get upset, but the police said there were some irregularities with Daddy's autopsy. They want to question me at the police station."

"Question you?" Sarah said, confused. "Why?"

Mrs. Minkus, red faced, gently smoothed her oldest daughter's hair. "They're just trying to figure out what's going on. There's nothing to worry about."

45

Joe was shocked. It almost sounded as if the police considered Mrs. Minkus a suspect.

"Mommy, don't go," Tori cried, throwing her arms around her mother's neck. Mrs. Minkus hugged her back.

"It's okay, honey. Mommy will be back in time for dinner—I promise." She turned to her oldest daughter and said, "Everything is going to be fine. I called Sid. He's going to meet me down at the station, and Marian is going to come to stay with you girls."

Sarah, however, couldn't stay calm. "They're taking you in a police car—like a criminal!" she almost shrieked.

Chet shot up from his seat and walked over to the police officers. Joe rushed after him. Chet usually gave the impression of being a big, sweet, teddy bear, Joe knew, but with his egg-like head and furious scowl, he resembled a shaved grizzly now.

Joe caught up with Chet just as his friend was confronting the two police officers. "What's the idea, upsetting them like this?" Chet growled. "Don't these girls have enough problems without your treating their mother as if she's guilty of something?"

Chet's hands were clenched into tight fists. Joe put a restraining hand on his friend's arm and felt the muscles there tense, as if Chet were ready to take a swing at one of the cops.

The detective didn't know Chet and clearly

didn't like his looks. He took a step back, his right hand slipping under his jacket. He was going for a gun in a shoulder holster.

Chet's shaved head must have thrown Con Riley, also, because the patrolman reached for his gun, too.

Chapter

6

"CHET!" JOE BARKED. "Get hold of yourself!"

Joe grabbed both of Chet's arms now and
shouted in his friend's ear. "Just think about it.
You won't be doing Sarah or anybody else any
good if you're taken downtown, too."

Frank Hardy moved up and laid a hand on
Chet's shoulder. For a long, tense moment Chet's
face was frozen in a scowl, then Joe's words sank
in. Chet wouldn't be able to infiltrate the Bootstompers if he was in jail for assault.

"Okay, Joe," he said, then addressed the officers again. "But why? Why are you treating Mrs.
Minkus like a suspect?"

"Did I say she was a suspect?" Riley answered.

"You already took her statement," Frank
pointed out, "and now you're taking her in for

questioning. And what's this about irregularities in the autopsy? Minkus died of electrical shock, didn't he?"

"Didn't I tell you and your brother to stay out of this case?" Riley answered sharply.

"Excuse me, but Sarah is our friend," Frank said. "And in spite of her father's radio personality, I don't want anyone to forget all the good he and his wife did."

"Settle down, Frank," Riley said. "Mrs. Minkus seems like a very nice person, but we still have to question her."

"I don't understand," Frank pressed. "She can't possibly have electrocuted her husband."

"The autopsy did show that Ron Minkus died from electrocution...." Riley said in a steady voice. "But he was also being poisoned to death slowly."

The Hardys and Chet stood stunned for a long moment. Then Judy Minkus reappeared, wearing a long wool coat. She seemed to notice Chet's thug disguise for the first time. "Sarah and Vanessa introduced Callie," she said. "But who are you?"

"Sorry, ma'am," Chet said, offering his hand. "I should have said something before. I'm Chet Morton—uh, I don't usually look like this—and this is Frank and Joe Hardy."

"You must be the young detectives I've heard so much about," she said. "Thank you for speaking up for me."

"You're welcome," Chet said. "We're terribly sorry about your husband's death."

"We're very sorry about everything," Frank said, glancing toward Officer Riley and his detective associate. "Especially this latest development."

"It seems the police come up with a new theory about Ron's death every few hours." Mrs. Minkus sighed, shaking her head. "The medical examiner's report shows that Ron had a near-lethal level of arsenic in his blood. Naturally they think I did it. I don't understand any of this. I just wish we could turn the clock back two days and start over."

"Mrs. Minkus," Frank said, "we want to help any way we can. I know this is hard for you, but would you mind if we searched your house a bit for any clues?"

"I could use any help you can offer," Judy Minkus replied, wrapping a scarf around her neck. "Look anywhere you like, but I've got to warn you, the police were very thorough.

"I'd better go," she murmured, looking back toward the family room. "I hate to leave the girls all alone—where is that Marian?"

"Mom, it's okay," Sarah said as she appeared holding Tori's hand. Sarah gestured around the room. "Do we look like we're alone? You really didn't even have to call Marian. We'll be fine."

Judy Minkus gave her children a hug and started for the door. "Sarah, don't forget to screen all calls on the answering machine—just in case crazy Cousin Dorothy or somebody from the press calls."

After her mother left, Sarah led the group back to the family room, where she sat on the couch with Tori, stroking her little sister's hair and wiping away her tears. "Mommy will be okay, Tori," Sarah said. "She'll be back soon."

"I know who Marian is," Vanessa said. "But who is this Sid your mom mentioned?"

"He's our lawyer, also a friend," Sarah answered. "My dad was always needing a lawyer." But the thought of her mother needing one brought Sarah's anger to the surface. "I can't believe my mom is a suspect," she fumed. "How dare they?"

"Sarah," Callie said, "just because they want to talk to her doesn't mean they think she did it."

"Who's crazy Cousin Dorothy?" Chet asked, changing the subject.

"Dorothy Minkus," Sarah answered. "She's my dad's cousin, the state senator. She always had a love-hate relationship with him. For the last few years, though, it's been more like hate-hate."

"Why's that?" Frank asked.

"Their politics clashed, among other things. They'd patch things up, then they'd meet at some family event, and there'd be a huge blowup."

"Cousin Dorothy doesn't like us," Tori said solemnly.

"Sometimes Cousin Dorothy is not very nice,"

Sarah added, putting her arm around her little sister's shoulders. "Why don't we go make some lunch?" The girls, followed by Chet, headed toward the kitchen. Frank asked Sarah if her dad had an office in the house.

"Top of the stairs, make a left. It's the third door on the right," she directed.

As Frank and Joe walked up the elaborate wooden staircase, they heard a little voice behind them saying, "I wanna help."

Frank turned to see Tori. "Tori, why don't you help Sarah make lunch?" he suggested. "I'll bet Callie will give you a cookie."

"I don't want a cookie, I wanna help," Tori insisted, and followed them into her father's study.

Frank had expected Ron Minkus's office to be as messy as his show was rowdy, with piles of paper scattered around and loud posters tacked to the walls. Instead, it was lined with dark wooden shelves neatly packed with books and magazines. There was a comfortable leather reading chair and brass lamp in one corner and a beautifully crafted mahogany desk facing a wall of windows, which framed a view of the snow-covered neighborhood.

"What a killer office," Joe said.

Frank switched on the desk lamp and began a systematic inventory of everything on the desktop. There wasn't much left but empty folders and a few family photos. "Mrs. Minkus was right about the police being thorough," he noted.

"They could have missed something," Joe said. "You take the shelves, I'll take the desk."

"What do I take?" Tori asked.

Frank thought for a minute and smiled at the little girl. "Tori, I have a very important assignment for you," he told her. "Do you think you can handle it?"

Tori nodded solemnly as Frank squatted down in front of her. "We're too big to see what's underneath things, so we'd like you to check under everything in this room that has a bottom." Tori, pleased to be helping, immediately began crawling around on her hands and knees.

As Joe rattled through the desk drawers, Frank began taking books off the shelves and methodically thumbing through their pages. Joe asked, "Why are you looking inside the books? Shouldn't you be looking between—or behind—them?"

"I'm doing that, too," Frank replied. Moments later a piece of paper fluttered to the floor. *"This* is why I check inside books," he said, bending to pick up the note. As he read it, he blushed and stuffed it back where it came from.

"What was it?" Joe asked.

"Never mind," Frank muttered.

"Come on, Frank," Joe insisted.

He walked over to Joe and whispered out of Tori's earshot, "It was a note from Mrs. Minkus to Ron. Really personal, okay?"

53

"Oh." Joe nodded.

"Even if it's nothing we can use, it does prove that Minkus sometimes slipped things in his books," Frank said, going back to his search.

"What's this?" Tori asked, holding up a big ball of dust.

"That's called a dust bunny," Joe answered. "Don't worry about it."

"What's this?" she continued, holding up a paper clip.

Joe turned to her and said, "Tori, why don't you go downstairs and make lunch with your sister?"

Tori's lower lip began to quiver. Frank, wincing at the thought of more tears, gave his brother a stern look. "I'm sorry, Tori," Joe apologized. "That's a paper clip—and keep up the good work."

Joe searched the files in the desk drawers while Frank worked his way up to the top shelf. A few minutes later Joe announced, "Nothing. Not a single clue. If there was anything here, the police have it."

"Joe, why don't you take the other set of bookshelves," Frank suggested. "We've got to check everywhere."

Frank and Joe paged through book after book. Then, as Joe pulled a particularly hefty volume off the shelf, he gasped, "Hey, Frank, check this out." Behind the book Joe had just pulled out, built into the wall, was a small door.

"Do you think we should open it?" Joe asked.

"Sure," his brother said. He turned the latch and flipped open the door.

"Cigars," Joe said. "It's a humidor." They had stumbled across Ron Minkus's secret stash of Cuban cigars. Joe shut the door of the little climate-controlled cabinet and started to check more books.

"Tori, where are you?" Frank asked. "How's your search going?" As he turned to survey the room, he saw the little girl's legs sticking out from under the reading chair. When she wiggled out, she held up a thin black leather case with an elaborate silver lock.

"I found this in the back of Daddy's big chair," she said.

"How did we miss that?" Joe wondered aloud as his brother got down on his back to look under the piece of furniture.

Frank slid out from under. "The rear bottom seam is actually a pocket," he said. "There's nothing else in there."

"Good girl," Joe said, picking the little girl up and swinging her around, much to her delight. "We never would have found this without you."

"Let's go ask Sarah if she knows what it is," Frank said. He picked up the case with the heels of his hands, taking care not to leave any fingerprints on it, and the three of them headed down to the kitchen.

Sarah, Chet, and Vanessa were all seated comfortably around the big kitchen table. In front of them was a huge pile of sandwiches already under attack by Chet. "Ready for lunch?" Sarah called.

Callie glanced at Chet and added, "You'd better hurry and grab a sandwich before they all disappear."

Frank sat down and showed Sarah the thin briefcase. "Have you ever seen this before?" he asked.

Sarah examined it carefully. "No, I don't think so. Where did you find it?"

"Tori found it in a secret pocket in your dad's reading chair," Joe answered, patting the beaming little girl on the head. "She was a big help."

"Let's open it," Sarah suggested.

"Isn't it locked?" Joe asked.

"So, we'll cut it open," Sarah replied.

Frank frowned. "We should probably hand it over to the police intact. It might be an important piece of evidence."

"The police are questioning my mom, so I say let's open it now," she said, grabbing a knife from a drawer.

"Not so fast," Frank said calmly. "A straightened-out paper clip will do the job better."

Sarah put down the knife and brought Frank a paper clip. After a little probing and twirling with his makeshift tool, Frank popped the lock. Sarah started to grab at the contents. "Patience," Frank said. "Now I need a pair of tweezers and a large Ziploc storage bag." Once he had those, he used the tweezers to pull out a piece of paper. It was a letter addressed to Ron Minkus at a different address.

"That's where they lived before they adopted us," Sarah said, reading the envelope.

"I hope it's not another love note," Joe muttered quietly to his brother.

"Just the opposite," Frank said, carefully slipping out the letter from its envelope. He spread it on the table, taking pains not to smudge any fingerprints that might remain on the paper. Glued to the page in cut-out letters was a message:

I AM GOING TO MAKE YOU SUFFER!

Chapter
7

SARAH STUMBLED BACK as if the hate letter were a poisonous snake rearing up to bite her. Chet jumped up to catch her in case she fell. "What happened, Sarah?" he said. "Are you okay?"

Vanessa took one look at what was written on the paper and grabbed Tori's hand. "Let's go back and play with your dolls," she said.

"I wanna see that," Tori answered, pointing at the piece of paper. "It's a collage. Marian taught me how to make them."

Vanessa gathered up several sandwiches and got a box of juice out of the fridge. "Come on, Tori, we're going to have a picnic with all your dolls," she said. That was enough to distract the little girl from the pieced-together message.

"You come, too," said Tori, tugging on Joe's shirt.

"I'll be there in a minute," Joe promised.

Sarah stepped forward and reached out as if she wanted to tear the paper up. Joe put a hand on her arm to stop her. "Who would do something like this?" Sarah asked in a choked voice.

"Did the sheet you found in the mailbox look anything like this?" Joe asked.

Sarah shook her head. Frank continued emptying the leather case. There were more threatening letters, with postmarks up to fifteen years old—long before Minkus was married or had a major radio show.

"I don't get it," Joe said. "If someone hated your dad this long, why wait till now to kill him? It doesn't make sense."

"Maybe the person who wrote these notes isn't the same person who killed him," Frank pointed out. "These are more about making him suffer than killing him."

Sarah sank back in a chair with Chet standing protectively over her. "I don't know how much more of this I can take," she murmured. "It's bad enough that my dad got killed, but trying to find out why is another kind of torture. Then, to top it off, the cops think my mom did it."

"They'll change their minds after they see these letters," Joe said.

Sarah nodded hopefully. Frank and Joe carefully put the letters and case into a plastic bag. "We'll go back to Bayport headquarters now,"

Frank said. "If we find out anything more, we'll give you a call."

Chet rose and followed his friends to the door. "I'm coming, too."

Joe met his gaze squarely. "Only if you can keep your mouth shut when we talk to Con Riley."

Chet hesitated. "All right," he finally agreed. "I promise to keep quiet as long as you keep me clued in."

It was a clear afternoon, but Joe noticed some snow clouds forming in the distance.

"Looks like we might get some more snow later," he said. "You drive, Frank." He tossed the keys to his brother. The ride back to Bayport passed quickly. As Frank looked for a spot to park the van in the police headquarters lot, Joe spotted Mrs. Minkus coming out of the building. She got into a double-parked car, which quickly pulled away.

"Good," Chet said. "They must've cleared her."

"Not necessarily," Frank said. "She could still be a suspect, but they may not have enough to hold her." They walked straight to the front desk of the station, where a dour sergeant glared at them.

"Frank and Joe Hardy for Officer Riley," Joe said. "We may have some evidence in the Minkus case."

After mumbling into the phone for a moment,

the sergeant hooked a thumb over his shoulder toward the squad room. "He said you know where to find him."

If Con Riley appeared tired, his desk appeared exhausted. There were at least ten empty paper coffee cups leaving rings on piles of paper. Riley was massaging his face with his hands as the boys walked up to him. He raised his eyes and said, "What have you got, boys?"

Frank handed Riley the bag containing the letters and the briefcase.

"Was this open when you found it?" the police officer demanded.

"No, but we didn't touch anything," Frank reassured him quickly. "I used tweezers to hold the letters and a paper clip to open the lock."

"Where'd you find this?" he said.

"In Minkus's office. Actually we didn't find it, his daughter did," Joe said.

"When?" Riley barked.

"This afternoon," Frank answered.

"Must be a plant," Riley growled. "We had people going over that office with a fine-tooth comb yesterday."

"Maybe their comb needs some new teeth," Joe muttered. Riley was too busy unfolding the first letter to note his remark. As he read the letter, his mood seemed to lighten.

"Maybe we can find some fingerprints on this note," he said. "Sorry to jump all over you guys, but with all the media attention this case is getting, everybody is going crazy here. Even the chief."

"Have you cleared Judy Minkus?" Joe asked, taking advantage of Riley's momentary lapse of grouchiness.

"You know I can't comment on that, Joe," Riley said, rubbing his face again. "Minkus had been poisoned over a long period of time. That had to be done by someone with regular access to his food."

"Do you have any other leads?" Frank pressed.

"We're checking everywhere, from disgruntled ex-employees to anyone he may have offended," Riley said, and shook his head in disgust. "Do you have any idea how tough it is to find the killer of a man who just about everybody had a reason to hate? I haven't gotten any sleep since before the murder."

"Maybe you should find a closet to take a nap in," Joe suggested with a smile.

"I just may do that," Riley answered. "Keep me posted if you hear anything else."

Frank, Joe, and Chet left the police station and got into the van. "Chet," Joe suggested, "why don't you call Mr. Pizza and order a couple of pies? Then call Sarah's house and ask her and the girls to meet us there."

Chet picked up the cellular phone and dialed.

"Don't you need the phone number?" Frank asked.

Chet raised his eyebrows. "For Mr. Pizza? Are you kidding? I have it memorized."

Chet ordered two large pizzas with the works, then called Sarah. After a brief conversation, Chet reported that Mrs. Minkus was back at home and that Marian, who showed up just after they left, would drop the girls at Mr. Pizza.

"I'm starving," Joe admitted as they pulled up to the pizza parlor. "We never did get any of those sandwiches, did we, Frank?"

The three boys were halfway through their first slices when Sarah, Callie, and Vanessa joined them. Frank went up to the counter and asked for more paper plates and another round of sodas. Their friend Tony Prito wasn't working that day, and the pizza wasn't quite as good as usual.

"I'm not very hungry," Sarah said.

"Sarah, you didn't eat any lunch," Vanessa reminded her. "It's not going to help if you pass out from hunger. Try to eat a little, please."

"Yes, Mother," Sarah said to her friend, smiling. She took a small slice and nibbled at it.

A couple of slices later, once he felt pleasantly full, Joe addressed Sarah. "I know we've asked you this before, but can you think of anyone who might have wanted to harm your dad? Was there someone he really insulted—or maybe fired?"

"Ron Minkus was an 'equal opportunity offender,'" she said. "I'm sure you've heard that. It was his unofficial slogan." She thought for an-

other second and added, "There was this producer he fired a few months back. He had
worked at the station for only a few months,
though, before he messed up."

"Can you remember his name?" Joe asked.

Sarah shook her head as she nibbled at her
pizza. Meanwhile Chet, sitting next to her, took
a huge bite of his fourth slice. Vanessa reached
into her bag and pulled out ten or twelve cas-
sette tapes.

"Look what we brought you," she said to Frank
and Joe. "The best of Ron Minkus. Since you
weren't regular listeners, we thought you might
find some clues by going through his shows."

"Some of them go back to when he was in
college in Burlington, Vermont," Sarah added.
"Dad was a lot sillier back then. He developed
his hard edge later."

"I can hardly wait to listen to them," Chet said.

"The funeral service is tomorrow morning at
nine," Sarah said. "You're all invited if you want
to come."

Joe blinked and said, "That was fast."

"Actually, if the police hadn't hung on to him
for so long, it would've been today," Sarah explained. "Mom and Dad are Jewish, and in the
Jewish faith the funeral takes place as soon as
possible. Then there are seven days of mourning.
It's called sitting shiva."

"If you're Jewish, why do you have so many
Christmas decorations?" Joe asked.

"Tori and I aren't Jewish," Sarah replied. "We were both baptized, so my parents decided to let us make our own choices about religion. I'm probably going to convert, but Tori is too young to make a decision like that. Besides, what almost six-year-old would give up Santa?"

Glancing at her watch, Sarah pushed back her chair and said, "I really should get back home."

Joe paid for the pizza, and they all went out and piled into the van. On their way to drop Sarah off, she pointed out Marian's house. "It's right on the border of Clearpoint and Bayport," she said.

After leaving the girls at their respective homes, Joe slipped one of the Minkus tapes into the van's tape player. Ron was interviewing a smooth Hollywood writer about his latest sci-fi novel. The man was very full of himself, until Minkus finally cut in. "I'm really confused by your style," he said. "It reads exactly like Graham Kilgore."

"Wha—who?" The big star seemed to stumble.

"He's a very talented, unknown writer. His books sell about a tenth of what yours do," Minkus said. "But my favorite gumshoe, Marian, turned up a really interesting paper trail. It seems your agent sends Kilgore a third of your payments. Could that be because he's ghostwriting for you? Doing the real work on your books?"

"How did you—I mean, yes, I have enjoyed

some professional help in polishing my work, but—"

"For me, buddy," Minkus interrupted, "your work has always been like that of a hammy actor. You merely acted the role of an author—and you did a pretty lousy job of it, too."

"Whoa!" Joe said. "Is that for real?"

Behind the wheel, Frank nodded. "Sure, the story was all over the papers after this show."

"You don't remember that this guy wrote whole books for you?" Minkus's voice continued. "Hey! Get us some oxygen in here. Our guest is suffering from major memory loss."

"I told you he was funny," Chet said, laughing at the DJ's tirade. "Funny and sharp."

"I guess we should add that writer's name to our growing suspect list," Joe said.

"Don't forget we have to check up on that producer, too," Frank reminded his brother, who jotted down a quick note.

The next tape was marked simply D.M.

"That probably stands for Dorothy Minkus," Joe suggested. He punched the Play button. It was indeed a show devoted to an interview of his cousin.

"So, Dorothy," Minkus said, "in twenty-five words or less, why should we make you a state senator?"

The candidate launched into a very slick little speech—an underhanded attack on immigrants that secretly played on people's worst fears and hatreds.

"It's not a question of racism," Dorothy said smoothly. "I just don't think it's fair to ask people to live in a culture where they don't fit in—"

"Except as nannies for fat-cat politicians who won't pay the wages an American would ask for the job," Minkus interrupted.

"You sound a little soft today, Ron," Dorothy Minkus shot back. "That's not like you."

"Dorothy, my dear, I just have a way of seeing through your arguments," Ron replied. "No matter how you sugarcoat it, racism is racism."

"You're just saying that because your wife made you adopt those two little girls," Dorothy said.

Ron Minkus's voice suddenly went as cold as steel. "I'd advise you to leave my family out of this," he said.

"Why should I?" she said. "It's my family, too."

"Because your family laundry is a lot dirtier than mine," Minkus said. "Why don't we talk about how your folks committed you to a mental hospital when you were seventeen?"

"Yikes!" Joe burst out. Frank hit the Pause button on the recorder and pulled the van over to the side of the road so he wouldn't be distracted. When the tape started again, Dorothy Minkus had completely lost her cool and was screaming at her cousin the DJ.

Minkus was screaming louder, though. "What really makes me sick is the fact that you're such a phony," he said. "Without all the speeches your handlers feed you, you wouldn't have a thing to say."

There was a snarl from Dorothy, then Minkus suddenly yelled, "Get that witch out of here—she threw a cup of coffee at me!" From the uproar that followed, it was obvious that Dorothy did not leave the studio without a struggle.

Frank switched off the tape and said, "Guess her name goes to the top of our list."

"Maybe," Chet said. "But we still need to get a line on the Bootstompers, and there's no time like the present. You might as well drop me at the Stop-n-Save."

The Stop-n-Save was a scruffy strip mall on the outskirts of town with a games arcade that was the Bootstompers' main hangout.

Chet, Joe, and Frank had agreed on a plan in advance. Frank would stay in the van by the curb with the engine running. Joe would get out and act as backup while Chet made contact with the Bootstompers.

They drove through progressively shabbier neighborhoods until they were a block from the Stop-n-Save. Frank pulled over, and Chet jumped out of the van. His heavy boots made splashing sounds on the slushy street as he stared walking.

The Hardys held their position until Chet had almost reached the strip mall. Then Frank turned and drove onto the cracked concrete parking apron.

"Where should I drop you?" Frank asked.

"The Chicken Pit," Joe replied. It was a fast-food joint next to the arcade. Lots of shaved-headed goons were hanging around both store-fronts.

Joe opened his door and stepped down. Out of the corner of his eye he could see Chet talking with a few of the thugs.

"Yo, pretty boy!" A hulking specimen pushed away from the wall where he'd been leaning. Stubble showed on his head, and crumbs of something were caught in his mustache. He headed straight for Joe. "Yeah, I'm talkin' to you! This is Bootstomper turf. You wanna go through here, you got to pay a tax."

A hand suddenly grabbed the back of Joe's coat and spun him around. He was looking straight into Chet Morton's glaring face.

"Yeah," Chet said. "And pretty boys like you belong to the top tax bracket."

Joe realized that Chet was trying to kill two birds with one stone: He could impress the Boot-stompers *and* let Joe off a little easier at the same time.

What Chet didn't realize was that the guy with the grubby mustache did not like his cutting in.

Mr. Mustache was showing his displeasure by swinging a big fist at the back of Chet's head!

Chapter

8

SORRY, CHET, Joe thought as he braced himself and gave his friend a shove. Chet flew off to the side, away from the thug's sucker punch. Joe came in under Mr. Mustache's swing and rammed a fist into his belly.

The breath came whooshing out of the big guy, and he folded in the middle. One down, twenty or so to go, Joe thought, watching the gang members converge on him. One guy had a baseball bat. Some had knives; some had brass knuckles. Well, I took care of Chet, Joe thought, but who's going to take care of me?

At that instant Joe felt a heavy hand grab the collar of his coat. Was Mr. Mustache back in the fight? No, it was Chet, doing a good impersonation of a Bootstomper. Too good an impersonation . . .

"Nobody pushes *me* around," Chet snarled. "Why don't you get your pretty face out of here?"

Chet grabbed the seat of Joe's pants with his other hand. Before he had time to react, Joe was airborne, hurtling toward the van. He landed inside hard enough to make the whole vehicle rock. Then Frank put his foot on the gas, and they took off.

"Wh-what about Chet?" Joe wheezed, catching his breath.

Frank glanced in the rearview mirror. "He's exchanging high fives with your other dancing partner. I guess he's a Bootstomper now."

"I think Chet really enjoyed throwing me," Joe muttered, wincing as he touched his chest and stomach, which felt pretty banged up.

Frank only shrugged. "Well, maybe you shouldn't have ridden him so hard about his new haircut."

After a long soak and a hot meal, Joe pronounced himself as good as new. He was sitting in the living room watching a Christmas special on TV as Frank headed for his father's office to dig up more background information on Ron Minkus.

The phone rang just as Frank was passing the kitchen. He went in and answered it. Callie was on the line. "I've decided to go undercover," she announced.

"First Chet, and now you," Frank complained. "I didn't think you were serious about that."

"I was out shopping and noticed a flyer in the health food store," Callie said. "WAM is having a meeting tonight to recruit new members. It's the perfect chance for me to check them out."

"Okay," Frank answered. "Do you want me to come with you?"

"I don't think so, Frank," Callie said. "The *W* in WAM stands for *Women*. Somehow, I don't think you'd pass." She chuckled. "The only danger I'm facing tonight is getting out of the house without my mother seeing me."

"I could give you a ride to the meeting," Frank said.

"It's only four blocks away, at the Java Joint on Sagamore Street," she said. "But you can pick me up afterward and I'll fill you in. According to the flyer, it'll be over at ten o'clock. Could you meet me then?"

Frank agreed. No sooner had he hung up than the phone rang again. This time it was Chet, reporting his progress as a Bootstomper.

"I played a lot of video games, ate tons of greasy chicken, and met Bobby Hadrava," Chet said. "He shot his mouth off about all kinds of things, but he didn't mention Ron Minkus."

"You can't expect to get that lucky on your first day," Frank said. "At least they accepted you."

"Yeah, as a fellow knucklehead." Chet paused.

"Remember when Joe suggested you guys go undercover with me?"

"Sure," Frank said. "We agreed it wouldn't work."

"That's right," Chet said. "But my new pal Bobby asked if I knew anything about electronics. I told him I didn't, but I was tight with two guys who did."

"Joe and me," Frank said.

"Exactly," Chet agreed. "He wants to meet you. The sooner the better. What are you doing tonight?"

"I have to pick up Callie at ten, but that's not for hours." Frank frowned. "Why do you think he needs an electronics expert?"

Chet was silent for a moment. "He wouldn't say, but somehow I doubt he needs help programming his VCR."

"We'll pick you up in a few minutes," Frank said.

"Just don't look too clean-cut," Chet warned.

After Frank hung up, he filled his brother in on the latest developments.

Fenton Hardy passed by, overhearing their conversation. "Chet and Callie *both* going undercover? What are you two doing, starting your own teenage detective agency?"

"Everybody wants to help Sarah Minkus find out who killed her father," Frank explained. "We saw this group of women protesting Minkus at the mall. They're called Women Against Minkus.

73

Callie found out they're meeting tonight and went to check them out."

"Are you sure that's a wise idea?" Fenton asked.

"It didn't sound too risky," Frank said. "And *we* certainly couldn't infiltrate them."

"I don't know, Frank." Joe smirked. "I'll bet Mom's pink angora sweater would look smashing on you."

Even Fenton had to smile at Joe's joke. He was worried about Callie, though, but after hearing she was at a busy coffeehouse, he retired to his study to read up on a case.

The brothers went upstairs to find some ratty old clothes for their meeting with the Bootstompers. "How does this flannel shirt look?" Joe asked his brother.

"Fine," Frank answered, pulling an old gray sweater over his T-shirt. "You should change your hairdo, though, 'pretty boy,'" Frank suggested. "It's a little too clean-cut. Maybe some of Mom's gel would help."

"Oh, come on, Frank," Joe said.

"Would you rather just shave your head like Chet?" Frank said. "I could get some shaving cream."

The Hadrava place was the most run-down building on a street lined with ramshackle houses. There was a time when most people in the area had worked at the nearby mill. When the mill closed, all the jobs, along with the neighborhood's sense of pride, vanished.

As the Hardys pulled up a block from the house, Chet warned them about Bobby. "He's obnoxious, and he's got an awful temper. Try not to punch him out, okay, Joe?"

The three walked down the block to the side door of the dilapidated house. Chet knocked until the paint-chipped door swung open to reveal a snarling pit bull. Pulling back on its chain was a young guy who was the human version of the dog: scruffy and mean.

"These are the friends I told you about," Chet said, gesturing toward Frank and Joe. "Frank, Joe, meet Bobby Hadrava," Chet said.

Hadrava gave them his most intimidating stare for a few seconds, then, after tying the dog's leash to a sagging porch post, he led them inside. "Chester here says you guys are good with electronics—that right?"

"We know our wires," Frank answered.

They followed Hadrava through a small, dark kitchen. "Bobby!" they heard a woman shout. "I don't want none of your hoodlum friends messing up my living room. You take 'em down to the basement. You hear me?"

Bobby's big, bald head reddened.

"You hear me?"

"Yes, Mother," he snapped.

Frank stifled a grin. So here's the big, tough

75

head Bootstomper, he thought. Still living with his mommy.

Bobby led them to a dank basement. Warped wooden paneling hung off the walls in several spots. A ratty carpet covered most of the cement floor. There was a sagging couch, matted with dog hairs, against one wall, and a pile of gasoline cans in one corner. The place smelled like a combination of gas station and badly kept kennel.

Slouching on the sofa was a skinny, tight-faced guy whose cue-ball haircut had grown out in a reddish fuzz. Frank noticed acid burns on his hands.

"Chet didn't tell us much about what you're looking for," Frank began.

"That's 'cause I didn't tell him." Hadrava nodded to the other Bootstomper. "This is Sparks."

The runty Bootstomper stood up and said, "I'm the armorer for this organization."

Hadrava pointed to a rickety card table and some folding chairs. "Take a load off," he said. "I assume Chester here has informed you of our agenda. First of all, we don't like foreigners coming in and stealing jobs from real Americans like ourselves. Somebody has to stop these people," Hadrava said. "They're ruining our neighborhoods and polluting the gene pool."

Frank thought this all sounded familiar. Dorothy Minkus had spouted a similar racist sentiment on "The Ron Minkus Show," only hers was better disguised. "I've heard some of your speeches,"

Frank said. "Weren't you on Ron Minkus's show a few months ago?"

Hadrava's fist came crashing down on the table. "Don't ever mention that pitiful excuse for a human being again!" he yelled. "He tried to stop our crusade."

"Crusade?" Joe asked.

"We're fighting to eliminate all non-Americans from our country," Bobby said. "Either they leave willingly, or we get rid of them by other means."

"How far do we go?" Frank asked, hiding his disgust.

Hadrava's face was dark with anger. "By any means necessary!" he shouted. "Now, are you with us or against us?"

Frank forced a smile to his lips. "I like what I hear," he said. "What do we do?"

"Show 'em your equipment, Sparksy," Hadrava said.

The so-called armorer dumped out a box of transmitters and timers onto the rickety table.

Frank poked at the equipment dubiously. "What do you want us to do with this stuff?"

"Make a better version of this," Bobby said, squinting at Sparks as he produced a box the size of a loaf of bread. Inside the box was a timer, wires, and a jar filled with clear liquid.

"We were going to use one of these to make a statement—a *loud* statement," the head Bootstomper said. "But nothing happened."

"I dunno what went wrong, Bobby," Sparks whined. "I followed the diagrams in *The Anarchistic Encyclopedia* exactly."

Frank knew the publication: It pretended to offer blueprints for all sorts of dangerous and illegal devices. "You can't be serious," he said. "Ninety percent of the stuff in that book is phony."

"No, it isn't," Sparks said, and picked up another, smaller box. "This is a motion detonator for blowing up cars. I got the plans from the encyclopedia. It even tells how to boil down a dynamite stick to soup—"

Frank stared at the box, his face pale. "You've got nitroglycerine in that thing?"

"Sure," Sparks blithely replied. "It was in the directions."

"I guess you missed the part about adding it only when you're ready to detonate." Frank's voice was hoarse. "Watch out, you're holding a live bomb there!"

Chapter

9

"DON'T MOVE," Frank said to Sparks.

Joe watched as his brother cautiously approached the would-be bomb maker. Nitroglycerine was very tricky. Even the slightest jiggle could cause an explosion. Sparks stood frozen, the detonator clutched to his chest.

Frank gently took the box, then sank to one knee, setting the box on the floor. He didn't even trust the rickety card table for his defusing job. He opened the package gingerly. "The nitro's in this tube?" he asked Sparks, pointing to a small vial filled with a thick, light yellow fluid.

Sparks nodded wordlessly.

Frank muttered, "At least it's cool in here."

Joe knew that nitro became even more unstable when it was warm. He was actually glad they were in a cold basement. Moving slowly, his fingers steady, Frank picked up the vial of nitroglycerine.

"That's all we're worried about?" Chet Morton said when he saw the size of the vial.

"It's enough to ignite all those gas cans if it blew," Frank said through clenched teeth. "Or take my hand off."

"So what are you going to do with it?" Hadrava asked.

"Throw it into your backyard, as long as there's nothing valuable back there."

Hadrava quickly opened a window, stood back, and said, "Okay, chuck it right through there."

Frank went to the window. He yelled, "Everybody down!" then tossed the tube out.

They all ducked and covered their heads as a loud roar erupted outside. They could hear the sound of dirt and debris splattering against the house and fluttering down into the yard. From upstairs came the cry "Bobby! What are you bums doing down there?"

Hadrava was ready to deck Sparks. "You're fired," he said. "We're getting a new armorer."

"Aw, Bobby," the runty Bootstomper began, "I just—"

His leader cut him off. "Today you nearly blow us up; the other day, when we needed it, you make a lousy—" He stopped himself, then offered his hand to Frank. "Fred, you seem like you know what you're doing. If you want the job, *you* can be our armorer."

"The name's Frank, Bobby, and thanks for the job," Frank said, gathering up the electronic items and putting them back in their box. "I think we can help you. We'll take these pieces home and check them out."

Joe took the box and started up the stairs. He glanced at Sparks. "If you have any nitro left, keep it in the freezer," he advised.

Frank indicated the pile of gas cans in the corner and said, "And you shouldn't store that stuff in the same place as bomb materials, unless you want to turn this house into a giant bonfire."

Hadrava followed them to the door and, after they promised to return the next day, clapped Frank on the back and said, "Glad to have you fellas with us."

"These guys are real wackos, aren't they?" Chet said once they were inside the van. "Sounds like they set up that bomb at the mall."

"A definite possibility," Joe agreed. "But I wonder if they have the smarts to have hot-wired Ron Minkus's microphone. What do we do with all that electronic stuff, Frank?"

"We take it to Riley," Frank said as his brother started the van. "Maybe the police can link some of the components to the bomb they found. Or to the microphone." He glanced at his watch. "But first we've got to pick up Callie—her meeting should be over just about now."

"I bet her undercover stint wasn't as hairy as ours," Chet said.

"I don't know," Joe said. "Have you ever tasted the coffee at the Java Joint?"

The three chuckled. To lighten the mood some more, Frank popped a Minkus tape in the player.

As they drove to the coffeehouse, they listened to some vintage Minkus rantings, this time about heavy metal music.

"These bands think they're so *baaaad,*" Minkus growled. "Ooooh, they're scary, boys and girls. I bet these drones were sponging off Mommy and Daddy till they lucked into a record deal. Yeah, they all lived at home in the suburbs, practicing their struts and sneers in front of the bathroom mirror. They probably still suck their thumbs and take their teddy bears to bed!"

"I'm not saying I disagree with him," Joe said, "but, boy, he could be nasty on these newer tapes. I was listening to some of his early shows at home. Sarah was right—he was sillier in his early radio days."

"Going nasty got him the top ratings, though," Chet said.

Frank shrugged and started to put another tape into the player. But as they rolled past the Java Joint, he saw something that made him freeze. It was a disheveled but familiar figure coming down the block after them. Joe must have glimpsed the same sight in the rearview mirror because he hit the brakes and said, "That couldn't be Callie, could it?"

The Hardys watched as she climbed into the back of the van. Callie, who never left even a corner of her shirt untucked, was wearing a black T-shirt and a leather jacket about six sizes too big. The rest of her ensemble featured cutoff shorts with ripped black tights underneath and big motorcycle boots. She had on heavy black eye makeup and bright red lipstick.

"Show's over, quit staring." Callie plopped down beside Chet. "We make a good couple, huh?"

"Where did you get all that stuff?" Frank asked a bit nervously.

"Don't worry, Frank," she said. "This isn't some secret side of me. I already had the cutoffs and I ripped my ballet tights. The boots and jacket come from my friend Nancy's older brother."

"Oh. So how does WAM check out?" Frank asked.

"I think most of them wouldn't hurt a flea," Callie said. "Only one of them, Sandy, seemed like she could be dangerous."

"They all seemed pretty dangerous Saturday," Joe pointed out.

She nodded. "They really hated Minkus, but I don't see them trying to kill him. They're vegans, you know."

"Vegans?" Joe repeated. "Sounds like something from a science-fiction movie. Is it anything like pod people?"

"Sort of," Chet said. "It's vegetarians."

"Oh, vegans go further than regular vegetarians," Callie explained. "Besides not eating meat, they don't eat any animal by-products, like milk or cheese." She looked down at her clothing. "They almost threw me out of the meeting when I turned up in a leather jacket and ordered a cappuccino. I had to tell them the jacket was borrowed, which was true, and that my cappuccino was made with soy milk, which I admit was a lie."

Joe laughed. "Sounds like a great club."

Callie held up a hand. "You haven't heard the best: They like the name WAM so much they don't want to change it just because Minkus died. So they conveniently chose another word that began with the letter *M*. Now they're Women Against Meat."

Joe rolled his eyes. "Maybe they should be called WWTMTOTH—Women with Too Much Time on Their Hands."

"Hey, how about fewer one-liners and more info about this Sandy?" Frank said.

Callie replied, "Well, she has purple hair, she's loud, she's obnoxious—and she did seem a little bit crazy, to tell you the truth."

"How so?" Joe asked.

"She was the only one who wanted to keep the

name Women Against Minkus," Callie answered. "She said he got what he deserved and she hoped his death was painful."

"Did you get her last name?" Frank asked.

"WAM doesn't believe in last names," Callie said. "Why should a woman be named after her father?"

"So we can identify her," Frank said. "Okay, let's drive you undercover agents home." After dropping Chet and Callie off, the Hardys drove to the police station.

As they pulled up in front of the building, Con Riley was coming down the stairs. He gave them a quizzical look as they approached. "For me?" he said, poking at the carton of electronic components.

"Transmitters, timers, gauges—bomb-making equipment," Joe explained.

"We got it from the Bootstomper honcho, Bobby Hadrava," Frank added.

Riley started back up the stairs and said, "What's a little more overtime?"

After hearing how they had targeted Bobby Hadrava, Con asked, "How would you feel about wearing a hidden transmitter?"

"Why don't you just go arrest them?" Joe said.

"From your description, the only incriminating evidence at the house would be the gas cans, which means the Bootstompers know how to make simple firebombs. Even this box of stuff means nothing, unless it's hooked up and ready to blow."

"You want us to make them a bomb?" Frank asked incredulously.

Riley shook his head. "No. I need you to let Hadrava incriminate himself and the gang on tape."

The Hardys agreed to the plan. After arranging to meet Riley after the funeral the next day, they went home to catch some much-needed sleep.

It was almost midnight when they got home. "I'm going straight to bed," Joe said, but their dad greeted them at the door and kept them up a bit longer.

"I talked to some people and got a name for you," Fenton said. "The fired producer is a guy named Hal Peters. And guess what? He's got an arrest record. Mostly disorderly conduct, but there is one assault and a harassment charge."

"What a case," Frank said. "Every time we seem to be making progress, another suspect crops up. Have the police talked to Peters?"

"He's gone missing," Fenton said. "No one has seen him for a few days."

"Maybe he killed Minkus and is on the run," Joe said.

"Maybe," Fenton said. "Peters seems to be unstable. Even if he's not the murderer, he could be dangerous. So be careful."

"Too many suspects," Frank mumbled as he and Joe headed upstairs. "Some of them go back fifteen years. We just don't have enough information."

The insistent bleeping of his alarm clock roused Joe Hardy at seven the next morning. He glared blearily at the clock until he remembered why he had to get up so early—the Minkus funeral. Joe padded down the hall to the bathroom, expecting to find that Frank had beaten him to the shower.

The bathroom was empty, and so was Frank's room. His bed hadn't even been slept in. A quick search and Joe noticed a light on in their father's office. Frank was slumped over the desk asleep. A computer modem was on, and so was the monitor screen. Frank had had a busy night.

"Hey." Joe tapped his brother on the shoulder. "Rise and shine."

"Huh?" Frank gasped as he jumped up. "What time is it?" he asked groggily.

"Time to get up." Joe peered at the screen. "What are you doing?"

"I was making a list of suspects and trying to look up some information on them." Frank stared out the window at the sunrise. "Guess I fell asleep."

Joe glanced at the list on the desk. "Why is Dorothy Minkus your number-one suspect and Hal Peters second? A guy who disappears after a murder would make the top of my list."

"Peters started working for Minkus about a

year ago. But we've got fifteen years of threatening letters." Frank rubbed his eyes. "The mike had been tampered with to kill Minkus. He was being slowly poisoned, and a bomb was found under the stage."

"That's a lot of hatred," Joe said.

"Long-term hatred," Frank added. "Each method took a lot of time and preparation. So I put the person with the longest grudge on top."

"I don't know," Joe said doubtfully. "I could grow a pretty big grudge in just a year." He tapped his finger on Dorothy Minkus's name. "You think she wrote the threatening letters?"

"I don't know about her," Frank replied. "And judging from the way he hid the letters, there's a lot we don't know about Ron Minkus, either. Some time last night I logged on to the news library and selected *Minkus*. It's still downloading articles."

Joe pulled up a chair as Frank began scrolling through the list of headlines. The most recent stories were on top, starting with Minkus's obituary from the paper the day before. "This might be interesting," Joe said, point to the headline. " 'Family Feud: Ron and Dorothy's Excellent Adventure.' "

"Let's print it out," Frank said, tapping on the keyboard. They went down the list, selecting more stories, until Joe glanced at his watch. "If we don't get moving, we're going to be late for the funeral."

The brothers showered and dressed in record time. Still knotting his tie, Joe ran downstairs and collected the thick sheaf of laser printouts. They jumped into the van, and Frank drove, stopping to pick up Callie and Vanessa.

The only sound that broke the solemn silence on the way to the funeral was the riffling of pages as Joe scanned the printouts. One headline in particular caught his eye: "Minkus Loses Election After Mental History Revealed." He showed it to Frank, who raised an eyebrow and said, "Leave that one on the top."

As they pulled into the funeral home parking lot, they saw a horde of photographers and TV crews surrounding the entrance. They parked the van, made their way through the media throng, and entered the chapel. Sarah, Tori, and Mrs. Minkus were sitting in the front row—all crying.

The Minkuses glanced up as a woman approached them. She was bundled in a thick, shapeless coat, her head shrouded in a large kerchief. She looked more like a bag lady than a mourner. The woman shoved a wrapped bouquet into Judy Minkus's hands, then quickly turned and headed for the door.

At first Mrs. Minkus appeared confused. Then she undid the wrapping and gasped, recoiling in horror.

Chapter

10

FRANK AND JOE rushed up to the Minkuses. The bouquet lay at Frank's feet. Through the torn wrapping, he saw withered black roses and a neon pink card with a sloppily lettered message: "Ron Minkus is where he belongs—SIX FEET UNDER!"

Joe spun in midstep and took off after the woman. Frank picked up the bouquet. Callie came over, read the message, and said in an urgent whisper, "That card is the same color as the WAM meeting announcement."

"Did you get a look at the woman?" Frank asked.

"Not really," Callie said.

Frank handed her the bouquet and note. "Go to the office and call Con Riley," he said. Then he took off after Joe in pursuit of the woman.

She was halfway down the block, but Joe was right on her heels. He managed to get a hand on her bulky coat, and the woman, thrown off balance, crashed into a parked car. Her kerchief flew off, revealing her purple hair. Obviously, this was Sandy.

"Get off me, you pig!" she shouted. "Get your filthy paws off me!" Sandy tried to slam a forearm against Joe's windpipe.

Joe dodged the blow so it landed on his shoulder. Holding on to one arm, he was trying to figure out how to stop Sandy without hitting her.

"Frank, want to give me a hand?" Joe called as Sandy tried to bite him.

"Callie called the cops," Frank said, grabbing Sandy's other arm. As he spoke, he heard the sound of approaching sirens. "Did you kill Ron Minkus?" he asked above the woman's snarled curses and threats.

"Drop dead," she spat. "Like that pig DJ!"

"I'd never think you had the guts for killing," Frank said coolly. "Tormenting a dead man's family is just about your speed."

Sandy became silent as a squad car pulled up. Frank told the officers what had happened, and Joe and he gratefully turned over their catch. One officer cuffed the girl while her partner headed for the funeral home to collect the evidence.

"Be careful," Joe warned the officer. "She bites." As the two brothers hustled back to the funeral home, Joe asked Frank, "You don't really believe she did it, do you?"

"I thought I might get her to blurt something out," Frank said. "To take credit if she was involved."

"If she knows enough not to blab," Joe said, "then why would she pull a dumb stunt with the flowers?"

"I have no idea," said Frank, "but I guess we have another suspect."

They joined their friends in a pew just as the service began. Chet, who had just arrived, gave them a what's-going-on look.

The rabbi came forward to begin reciting the *Kaddish*, the Hebrew prayer for the dead, but had to pause because of a big commotion at the door. It was State Senator Dorothy Minkus making her entrance. Newspeople, with cameras clicking and whirring and microphones outstretched, had crowded around her at the entrance to the chapel. She marched down the center aisle toward the front, accompanied by a hulking bodyguard, a thin, pale assistant, and a sharp-faced woman who seemed to be writing constantly in a notebook.

They noticed another woman in the front row, sitting quietly and holding Judy Minkus's hand. "That's Marian Brown," Vanessa whispered to Joe. "You haven't met her yet, have you?" Joe shook his head.

Dorothy Minkus sat apart from the rest of the

family. Frank noticed that she wore a blank expression throughout the service and didn't shed a tear.

As they left the chapel, Joe caught up with Sarah. "Who's that man with your cousin?"

"That's Jerry the Hammer, her bodyguard," Sarah replied. "Dorothy is using my father's death to get free publicity. She's blaming Dad's murder on 'a lawless climate created by joblessness and unlimited immigration.' She's also claiming she's had death threats against her. That woman following her around is a reporter who seems to believe everything Dorothy tells her."

"I guess it's politics as usual," Frank said.

"She's been too busy posing for the cameras even to speak to us," Sarah said, choking back tears. "Now we have to go to the cemetery for the burial."

Frank and his friends saw Sarah to the limousine where her mother was waiting. They promised to meet at her house for the reception and went to where they were parked. Chet had driven over himself, so they stood talking with him beside the van for a few minutes.

"Guess what, Chet?" Joe said. "Con wants us to go back and meet with Hadrava so we can catch him on tape shooting his mouth off about bombs."

"Can I wear the wire?" Chet asked.

"That will be up to the police," Frank said.

"What are you guys talking about?" Callie asked.

Frank filled her in on the Bootstompers' bomb-building program on the way to the Minkus estate.

"These are the jerks that do the dirty work for people like Dorothy Minkus," Vanessa fumed. "She talks about lawlessness and blames it on 'immigrant elements,' then those hoods attack foreign store owners. She makes the speeches—they plant the bombs."

Frank and Joe let Callie and Vanessa off in front of the Minkus house and went to park the van. As they walked back, Frank spoke up, "We've got business here. We have to interview Dorothy and Marian."

"I understand Dorothy, but why Marian?" Joe asked.

"She might inherit Minkus's radio empire," Frank said. "She could take over the show now, then eventually get promoted to his job and salary. It's big bucks."

"Okay," Joe said. "I'll quiz Marian, and you take on Senator Dorothy."

Frank was amazed at the stream of people filing into the house. For a man with so many enemies, it seemed Ron Minkus also had plenty of friends. The media had camped out in front of the house again and were attempting to interview anybody who'd slow down long enough to answer a question. The Hardys hurried past without a word.

Once inside, the two split up. Frank was a few feet from Dorothy Minkus and closing fast when Jerry the Hammer stepped into his path. "Senator Minkus doesn't want to be disturbed in her grief," he said.

"I'm a friend of Sarah Minkus," Frank said. "I just wanted to ask a few questions." The bodyguard continued to shield Cousin Dorothy as she glided away. Soon she was across the room talking to a familiar-looking man. Frank realized it was the mayor of Clearpoint and decided to try a different tack.

"Excuse me, sir," Frank said, approaching the mayor.

"May I help you?" he asked with a pleasant smile.

"I hope so, Mr. Mayor." Frank gave him his earnest student look. "I'm writing a story for my school paper on how Ron Minkus's life and death affected our community. Could you spare a few minutes?"

"Well, son," the mayor answered. "I'd be glad to share my feelings on Mr. Minkus, but this lady here could probably help you a lot more. She's his cousin, State Senator Dorothy Minkus. Senator?"

Dorothy's glance at Frank was dubious. The mayor of Clearpoint had been an ally in the last election, and Dorothy knew better than to alienate him. So she smiled as the mayor gave them a thumbs-up sign and walked away.

Dorothy's smile faded quickly, and she said to Frank, "What can I do for you, young man?"

"I was wondering, Senator Minkus," Frank asked in an innocent tone of voice, "why do you think someone would want to kill your cousin Ron?"

The senator's expression changed automatically to one of concern as she reeled off a standard answer. "Ron was an outspoken man. Certain lawless elements in our society, people who don't accept the give and take of democracy, are most likely to blame."

"I see," Frank said. "The murder must have been a great shock to you."

Dorothy nodded, concern still creasing her brow, and said slowly, "Yes, it was awful hearing the news. We were like brother and sister."

"I'm glad to hear you patched up your relationship," Frank said. "I heard it suffered after he revealed your stay in the mental hospital."

This time Dorothy Minkus had no stock answer ready. Her face flushed with fury, and she snapped, "Who are you, young man? And how dare you bring up that interview. That cost me an election, and it made Ron Minkus a big ratings star." She leaned forward and said, "A big, *nasty* star." Then turning, she strode off.

Meanwhile Vanessa had introduced Joe to Marian Brown. He got a warm handshake from

Ron Minkus's sidekick, who said, "So you're one of the young detectives Sarah mentioned. I hope you can solve this murder. It would really help Sarah and her family to come to terms with it."

"I guess you'll be going through some big changes yourself," Joe said. "Are you going to continue with the show?"

Marian reacted with horror to the question. "Of course not," she gasped. "I couldn't go on without Ron." She shook her head sadly. "He may have played a madman on the air, but he was truly a good guy in real life."

"Can you think of anyone in particular who might have wanted to harm Ron?" Joe asked.

"Joe, there are a lot of unstable people out there," she said. "For example, when we did the show at the mall, I saw this guy Ron fired glaring at us from the crowd. Hal Peters is his name. He produced the show, but not for long."

"Are you planning to stay around here?" Joe asked.

"To tell you the truth, I've decided to quit radio," she said. "And I think I'm going to leave this area."

"That's too bad," Joe remarked. "I know Judy, Sarah, and Tori really care about you."

Marian stared at the floor as tears filled her eyes. "I'll miss them," she said, "but I think I'd like to be with my real family for a while."

"Where's that?" Joe asked.

"Burlington, Vermont," Marian said, her eyes

fixed past Joe's shoulder. He turned to see what had distracted her and saw Dorothy Minkus storming across the room.

Joe focused back on his conversation. Burlington? Where had he heard the name of that town recently?

Then Marian was distracted again, this time by Judy Minkus, who was approaching them, obviously very upset. "Judy, what is it?" Marian reached out to steady her friend.

"Cousin Dorothy." Judy made the words sound like a curse. "She wants to use my front porch—*Ron's* front porch—to make one of her speeches."

"She's got a lot of nerve," Marian said.

"She said I owed her because I wouldn't let her speak at the funeral," Judy said, raising a shaky hand to her head.

"So what are you going to do?" Joe asked.

Judy's face hardened. "I'm not going to give her a soapbox," she said. "I asked her to take her little circus and leave."

Joe excused himself and went to find Frank. He found him in the entryway, chatting with Chet. When Joe told them what he'd heard about Cousin Dorothy, Chet's face grew hard and he said, "Somebody should take that woman and—"

At that moment there was an angry outburst in the next room. The boys turned to see some of the private security guards Judy Minkus had hired for crowd control asking Dorothy to leave as politely as possible.

"This is outrageous!" she said. "I have every right to speak. His wife tried to gag me at the funeral. She's just a Minkus by marriage. But *I* am a blood relative." She flashed a scornful glance at Tori and Sarah. "Unlike some of these people!"

Chet, overhearing this insult, was ready to explode. Frank tried to grab his arm, but Chet shook him off and walked right up to Dorothy's bodyguard. "Why don't you shut your boss up and get her out of here?" he growled. "We don't need to hear this garbage."

Hustling over to where Chet and the bodyguard stood toe to toe, Frank said, "Hey, Chet, calm down. It's not worth starting a brawl."

Chet was momentarily distracted by the sound of Frank's voice, just enough for Jerry the Hammer to sense an opening and demonstrate how he got his nickname. As Chet glanced away, the bodyguard yanked back his big right fist and punched Chet square in the face!

Chapter

11

WHEN THE BODYGUARD'S FIST connected, Chet crumpled to the floor in a heap, grabbing his face with both hands. The crowd went silent and Frank stepped up to the Hammer.

"Want to try that again—with somebody who's ready for it?" Frank challenged.

Sneering, the bodyguard took a swing at Frank, who ducked and wrapped his hands around Jerry's wrist. He turned his back on the big man to add some extra leverage. As he pivoted, Frank pulled down hard on Jerry's wrist and tossed the man in a classic judo throw. The Hammer went flying through the air and would have crashed into the front door if Chet hadn't thrown it open.

The Hammer was sprawled ingloriously on the front porch in front of the media army's cameras.

He got up slowly, brushing off his dark suit, as a tight-lipped Dorothy Minkus stomped out of the house and down the steps.

Inside there was dead silence for a moment, then a growing buzz of voices. A big group crowded around Frank to congratulate him. Chet gave him a high five. Sarah walked up to Chet, stood on her tiptoes, and planted a kiss on his cheek.

"Thank you," she murmured. "Thank both of you." When Sarah kissed him, Chet turned beet red.

"We'd better get some ice for that eye," Judy Minkus said, and beckoned Chet toward the kitchen.

"Looks like he's going to have a nice shiner," Joe said quietly to his brother.

As Chet followed Judy Minkus, Tori came up to him with her Malibu Mindy doll. "You're nice, and Dorothy's mean," the little girl said. Grinning, Chet took her hand and led her into the kitchen.

When Chet returned holding an ice pack over his eye, Joe glanced at his watch. "We should be getting over to meet Riley," he said. Frank, Joe, and Chet said their goodbyes and went out to the van. Chet left his car for Vanessa and Callie so they'd have a ride home later.

As they drove back to Bayport, Frank told Joe and Chet about his interview with Dorothy. "She's a real professional, very slick," he said. "I thought I might crack her facade by bringing up that hospitalization story. She claimed it cost her an election and made Ron a star." He glanced at Chet. "Apparently, that was when he learned the benefits of being nasty."

"Marian was a lot easier to talk to," Joe said. "She's not planning to take over the radio show, so there goes that theory. She said she was thinking of going home to Vermont." He shook his head. "Why does Burlington, Vermont, keep ringing a bell?"

"That's where Minkus started out," Chet said. "On the college radio station."

Frank gazed at the file of news stories they'd printed out that morning. "But from what we gathered," he said, "Minkus and Marian didn't hook up until some years after that."

Joe began leafing through the articles as Frank drove on. He glanced up as they reached downtown Bayport. "Hey, there's LaVerne's, Mom's favorite jewelry store." A guilty look passed across his face. "We never did get her a Christmas gift."

"I haven't gotten my mom anything, either," Chet said.

Frank didn't need to be reminded that Christmas was coming. The holiday traffic downtown was reminder enough. He glanced in his rearview mirror. "You know, guys," he said, "I think we're being followed."

Joe glanced out at his sideview mirror. "Where?"

"Hard to miss," Frank said. "It's that mud brown sedan. It was behind us in Clearpoint, and it's just turned up again."

They crawled along in stop-and-go traffic, the "mud-mobile" on their tail. "No way are you going to outrun him in this traffic," Joe said. "Why not turn the tables?"

Frank nodded and abruptly changed lanes, darting into a small opening. As the car pulled up beside them in the slow-moving traffic, the boys leaned over to catch a glimpse of the driver. Unfortunately, their pursuer was bundled up in a ski hat, sunglasses, and shapeless parka.

"Why don't you call Con," Frank suggested, and slowed enough to slide the van back in the next lane behind the mud-mobile.

As Joe punched the numbers into the cellular phone, the light changed and his brother followed the other car. Joe read the license plate number to Riley and told him where they were. "Looks like he's heading for the highway now," Joe said.

They chased the brown car up an entrance ramp. Frank had to cut in front of another car in order to merge behind the mud-mobile, which quickly began darting in and out of lanes. Frank kept the van close behind.

"Riley ran the license," Joe said. "It's Hal Peters's car." The mud-mobile suddenly swerved from the right to the middle lane. Frank jockeyed the van up on the right side of the car.

"Hang on both of you," Frank said. "He's trying to sideswipe us." The brown car suddenly lurched hard right. Frank managed to avoid a collision by swerving onto the snow-covered shoulder. As the van fishtailed, the phone flew out of Joe's hand and landed at his feet, disconnecting his call to Officer Riley.

The brown car shot ahead and Frank sped up. Moments later they could just make out the sounds of sirens behind them.

"I hope that's for us," Chet said.

"Frank," Joe said. "Marian Brown told me Hal Peters was at the mall on the day of the murder. Now look what he did. I guess I was right. He must be our man."

"I didn't see him, did you?" Frank asked. "I saw an unrecognizable person driving that car."

"Who else would—" Joe began, only to be interrupted by the phone ringing. "It's Riley, calling back," Joe said, a hand over the receiver. "He says just go to the station, they've got all available squad cars chasing Peters."

"Chasing Peters's *car,*" Frank corrected. "I hope they catch it. The next exit is Harborside. There are a million little sidestreets to ditch a car there."

As soon as the Hardys and Chet reached Riley's desk, the officer began briefing the boys on what would happen. Frank would be fitted with a transmitter to send signals to a police van down the block from the Hadrava house. The box of electrical bits and pieces was returned to them.

"The lab matched some of the components to the bomb in the mall," Riley said. "Now all we need is for you to get Hadrava to implicate himself." He drummed his fingers on his desk. "I'm a little nervous about sending you boys in there—"

"Then just send me," Chet offered. "I'm already a Bootstomper—"

Riley cut him off. "I'm afraid your undercover career has been grounded. And probably just in time, judging from that shiner you've got."

"B-b-but—" Chet spluttered.

"Son, I need parental permission before I can use a minor in a situation like this," Riley said. "I called your mom, and she nixed it immediately.

"On the other hand," he said, glancing at the Hardys, "your dad okayed the idea. In fact, he'll be in the surveillance van with us."

Then Riley took pity on the deflated Chet. "Okay, Chet, you have my permission to join us in the van."

"Well, that's better than nothing," Chet said.

Frank and Joe went over their story with Riley as a technician fitted Frank with the transmitter. They decided that if Sparks was on hand, they'd ask him how he put together the bomb that didn't go off at the mall. If that didn't work, they'd mention how much news coverage there was of

Minkus's funeral and hope Bobby would rise to that bait.

Riley promised the police would close in to make the arrests only after the Hardys signaled they'd left the house and were out of danger.

In the back of the van Frank and Joe changed into grungy outfits like the ones they'd worn the day before. Then they drove to Bobby Hadrava's place.

Bobby saw them pull up and immediately signaled them inside. He seemed to be in a much better mood than the day before. "How's it going, Bobby?" Frank said.

"Great. We got the place to ourselves today— and just wait till you see what we're gonna do tonight!" he said eagerly. Once they were downstairs in his headquarters, however, he tried to act like a leader of men. "So did you check those timers and detonators?" he asked gruffly.

Joe laid the box on the table. "You've got some stuff here that will work," he said, "depending on what you want to blow up."

"You don't have to worry about timers," Frank said. "If the timer doesn't work, you can still set off a bomb by remote control. Just rig a back-up detonator with some of the transmitters here."

Frank hoped that comment might lead Hadrava to question what went wrong with the bomb at the mall. The head Bootstomper only answered with a grunt, though. He acted distracted by a sheet-covered mass in the corner near the cans of gasoline. "Wanna see what we've got planned?" he asked.

"Sure," Frank answered.

Bobby yanked back the top half of the sheet to reveal a store mannequin with a head of dark brown hair. "Did you guys hear that Minkus burned a Santa doll at the mall the day he got fried?"

Frank's eyes narrowed. "Yeah," he said. "I heard there was a bomb—"

Bobby drowned him out. "This is a Minkus doll. We're gonna burn it on his family's lawn tonight," he said, picking up a propane torch and lighting it.

Frank was revolted. This was just petty cruelty, like Sandy's flowers, only flashier. "The guy's dead," Frank said. "Why bother his family?"

Bobby's face twisted into a snarl. "You know what color his kids are?"

"Who cares?" Joe retorted.

"The Bootstompers care!" Bobby roared.

"Careful with that torch," Frank said. "You've got a lot of gasoline down here."

"Don't change the subject," Hadrava barked. "Do I have to ask you again? Are you with us or against us?"

"Hey, we're with you," Frank said. "I just don't know about terrorizing women and children."

Bobby was ranting now and waving the torch around for emphasis. "Nits grow into lice!" he shouted, not noticing when the tip of the torch ignited a corner of the sheet that was still partly draped over the Minkus mannequin.

"Watch it!" Frank yelled, pointing at the small but growing fire. When he started to stamp out the flames, the tape holding the transmitter to his back gave way. The transmitter slid down and dangled out from under his T-shirt.

Seeing this, Hadrava raised the propane torch like a club, his eyes narrowing. "Hey! Who are you guys?"

Frank gave up on the fire, which by now had spread all over the sheet. "Let's get out of here, Joe." Together, they charged up the stairs.

Footsteps pounded after them. Whether Hadrava was trying to escape the fire or pursue them for a fight, Frank didn't know or care. He saw the side door and he saw Joe plow through it. Frank was three steps behind his brother when a powerful arm clamped around his throat from behind.

Frank raised his hands to break Hadrava's choke hold. Then he felt the whoosh of an explosion erupting from below. The next thing he knew, both he and Bobby Hadrava were flying through the air, propelled by a fireball that was rolling up the basement stairs.

Chapter

12

THE EXPLOSION THREW JOE to the ground. He looked around, expecting to find his brother right beside him.

"Frank!" he yelled. No answer. The whole ground floor of the house was in flames now. Joe's skin tightened from the heat as he went back to peer into the thick smoke. Something moved just inside the side door. "Frank?" he muttered, stepping in that direction.

His brother lay sprawled across the threshold with Bobby Hadrava on top of him. The Bootstomper's shaved head was scorched, and his leather jacket was smoldering, but he still had Frank in a choke hold.

Joe didn't have time to fool around. He kicked Hadrava in the ribs, and the head Bootstomper yelped in pain, his grip on Frank weakening. Joe grabbed Hadrava's jacket with both hands and hauled him off Frank, who staggered to his feet.

The Hardys both started dragging Hadrava to safety. They'd only gone a few steps when a police cruiser and van screeched to a halt in front of the house.

"What happened?" Riley yelled as he charged across the lawn followed by Fenton Hardy, Chet Morton, and several officers.

"This genius started a fire in a room full of old gas cans, then he tried to keep me in the house and strangle me." Frank jerked a finger at Hadrava, who lay flat on his face, coughing weakly.

"Frank, are you all right?" Fenton Hardy asked.

"Luckily he fell on top of me and got the worst of it," Frank said. "We should call an ambulance."

"Got one coming already," Riley reported. "And the fire department is on the way."

As they watched, the rest of the house went up in flames. Riley told the boys he had enough evidence on tape to bring Hadrava up on a number of charges. "I think we can rule him out as the murderer, though," Frank said. "These losers don't seem to have the technical know-how to have rigged Ron Minkus's microphone. They can barely tell the difference between a transmitter and a receiver."

Paramedics arrived to pick up Hadrava, and

firefighters began to battle the blaze. Joe turned to Con Riley and asked, "Did they ever catch Peters?"

Riley shook his head and said, "He got off the highway and left the car down by the docks in Harborside. We've got an APB out on him so it's only a matter of time before we catch up to him."

"Well, good luck," Fenton said, giving Officer Riley a friendly wave and turning to his sons. "Fellas, it's time to go home."

"Frank, Joe," Fenton announced somberly after they'd dropped Chet off and promised to call him later. "I know you've had a long day, but we still have a very important mission to accomplish. Something we've been ignoring for too long."

"What is it, Dad?" Joe asked a bit worried.

"Operation Christmas tree," Fenton said. "Your mom said if we don't get one, don't bother coming home."

The Hardys picked out their tree at a nearby garden center, then drove home. It was already dark out when they pulled in the driveway. Frank checked his watch and was surprised to see it was only four-thirty. It felt more like nine-thirty at night to him. He was exhausted and covered with soot from the explosion.

After reassuring their mom they were okay, Frank and Joe helped their dad put up the six-foot spruce tree. Laura Hardy then reminded her husband that he'd promised to take her Christmas shopping.

"Have a *great* time at the mall, Dad," Joe said with a wink. He waved to his parents, who said they'd be home for dinner.

"Let's go through the files and listen to some more tapes," Frank suggested to Joe.

They washed up and changed clothes, then got to work. Frank pored over their files while Joe popped a tape into the recorder. "You know, Con Riley didn't mention what happened with that girl Sandy," Joe said.

"No, he didn't," Frank agreed. "She seems like she'd be tough to crack, though. I doubt she's said anything yet." Frank held up a sheaf of papers, changing the subject. "There's some interesting coverage of Dorothy and Ron in here," he said.

"Such as?" Joe asked.

Frank was about to answer when the phone rang. "It's Chet," he said.

"I'll pick up the extension in the kitchen," Joe said.

"Guys," their friend said in a breathless whisper. "I called the hospital to check on Hadrava."

"How bad is he?" Joe asked.

"All the receptionist would say was he was under police guard," Chet said. "So I went there. I'm there now—on a pay phone. I told them I was Bobby's cousin, and I think my Bootstomper disguise helped convince them. Con Riley was in there questioning him so I waited until he finished."

"What happened?" Frank said. "Did Hadrava confess?"

"Not to the murder," Chet answered. "But he did admit planting the bomb in retaliation for Minkus having him arrested."

"Good work, Chet," Frank said. "We're looking into some of the other suspects, especially Hal Peters."

Before they hung up, Frank and Joe promised Chet they'd stay in touch and keep him informed on any new developments in the case.

"It seems pretty obvious that Peters is the murderer," Joe said. "Why else would he follow us and try to run us off the road?"

"We still don't know if it was Peters in the car," Frank said. Then he thought for a moment. "And even if it was, how did he know we were involved in this case?"

"I think he's been hanging around more than we realize," Joe said. "If he was at the mall the day of the murder as Marian Brown said, he could just as easily have been hanging around the Minkus house and seen us coming or going."

"In any case, he's at the top of our list now," Frank said. "Joe, I think it's time we paid a visit to Mr. Peters's home to see if he's shown up there yet."

Joe quickly checked the phone book for his

address, then they grabbed their coats and headed for the door.

Hal Peters's address was on a dead-end street in a rundown part of town. Frank found a parking space behind a junked car with a backseat with its stuffing and springs popped out. The seat was sticking halfway out one of the back doors. Peters's building was a six-story tenement with two rusty fire escapes running down the front. A small white-haired woman was sweeping the front steps as they walked up.

"Excuse me, m'am, but do you know Hal Peters?" Frank asked her.

The elderly woman straightened up and put her hand on her hip. Frank estimated her age to be eighty-plus and her height to be under five feet. "Now, you wouldn't be the police, would you?" she demanded in a thick Irish brogue.

"No, ma'am," Joe assured her. "We're Hal's nephews," he lied smoothly. "Our mom is his sister. She hasn't heard from him in a few days and she's really worried."

The old woman looked the two up and down and said, "Looks like you two stole all the good looks in the family. Why don't you look like him?"

"Luck of the Irish, I guess," Frank said.

The old woman laughed heartily and motioned for them to follow her into the building. "Name's Maeve. I don't know if I believe you rascals, but you tell a good story and I'll let you look around a bit."

The two watched as Maeve fumbled with Peters's door. When it finally swung open, they were greeted with the smell of rotting garbage. The late afternoon darkness made it difficult to see inside, so Joe tried turning the light switch. Nothing happened.

"Your uncle is behind on his bills, including his rent," Maeve said. "I've got some candles. Be right back." As she shuffled down the hallway, Frank and Joe entered the apartment.

"I don't think our boy has been home in a while," Joe noted, pointing to a batch of advertising circulars on the floor in front of the door. The brothers inched their way into the apartment, their eyes gradually adjusting to the darkness.

"What a mess," Frank muttered as he stumbled over a stack of old newspapers in the living room.

Maeve returned with two candles. As she handed them to Frank and Joe, she asked them to let her know when they were done so she could lock up.

"Will do, Maeve—and thanks," Frank said. The candles cast wavering shadows on the walls, making the already small apartment seem smaller and cavelike.

As Joe glanced through the circulars, Frank looked around the living room. "Anything interesting?" he asked his brother.

"Nah," Joe replied. "Let's see what's in here," he said, pointing toward a closed doorway. When he opened the door, the stench of garbage grew much stronger.

"It's the kitchen," Frank noted. They surveyed the tiny room in disgust. Food-encrusted dishes filled the sink, the garbage can was overflowing, and the floor felt as if it was covered in sticky, dried soda pop. Frank went to the half-open refrigerator and looked inside. The smell of spoiled milk was overwhelming. What little food there was on the rusty shelves was covered with green fuzz. "Nothing much in—"

"Whoa!" Joe said, dropping his candle on the floor. "Something just ran across my foot. And I don't think it was a cat."

Frank picked up his brother's candle and relit it with his. Joe had bumped into the trash can when he dropped his candle and knocked it over. An even fouler odor was released into the air.

Joe's eyes were actually tearing from the stench as he picked up the receptacle. But they suddenly focused wide when he spotted the label on something shiny amid the glop.

"Frank, come here." He gulped as he carefully grasped a small metal container by its edges and lifted it out of the trash between his thumb and forefinger. "I don't believe this."

Frank and Joe stared down at the container. The label was stained, but they could still clearly make out a skull-and-crossbones warning symbol and one word printed in unmistakably bold type underneath: Arsenic.

Chapter

13

"So, it was Peters who was poisoning Minkus," Joe said. "Maybe he got tired of waiting for the stuff to work and hot-wired the microphone. He probably *would* know how to do that."

"Watch it," Frank warned, handing Joe his handkerchief. "We don't want any of your fingerprints on that can."

Joe wrapped the container in Frank's handkerchief and pocketed the bundle.

"Who knows?" Frank speculated. "Peters may have bought the arsenic to poison whatever it was that ran across your foot. Besides, he hasn't worked with Minkus in months—so how could Radio Ron still have had so much of it in his system?"

Joe was stumped. "I don't know," he said.

"But let's go turn this evidence over to the police."

"They must have checked this place out already," Frank said. "Con Riley's going to love hearing how his people missed that can."

"They were probably in a hurry to leave," Joe said, waving a hand in front of his face. "I know *I* am."

They left the apartment right away, remembering to thank Maeve on the way out. "I'll tell your uncle you're worried about him, and he should call your mum," she said, and winked.

"Where *were* you boys?" Laura Hardy asked as her sons walked in the front door. "It's almost seven o'clock, and dinner is about to be served."

"Then I guess we're just in time." Joe grinned and gave her a kiss on the cheek. Frank excused himself and ran upstairs to phone the police in private.

Luckily, Con Riley was still at the station. "What it is, Frank?" he asked in a clipped tone.

"Ahhhh—" Frank realized that he didn't have the foggiest idea of how to explain their burglary of Peters's apartment. He decided to wing it. "I might have something about Hal Peters—"

Riley cut him off in midsentence. "Who told you about Peters?"

"You've got him?" Frank said.

"Somebody got him," Riley said, then paused. "He's dead, and it was definitely no suicide."

Frank wasn't sure how to respond.

"Isn't that why you're calling?" Riley said.

"Er, not specifically," Frank said. "How—when did he die?"

As Frank spoke, Joe came into the room and heard the tail end of his sentence. Joe made a come-on gesture with his hand, asking for the story.

Frank waved him off, still listening to Riley. "He was shot in the head," the officer said somberly. "The medical examiner estimates that it happened yesterday."

"That would be after the murder," Frank said. "Still, it couldn't have been Peters driving when we tailed his car."

"I had a crew go over that clunker again when the body turned up," Con said. "It was wiped clean—no prints, no trace of Peters. Now, what were you going to tell me?"

Frank took a deep breath. Now there were two murders under investigation. Best to tell the whole truth. "Joe and I were inside Peters's apartment today. We found a can of arsenic in his garbage. He could have been the one poisoning Minkus."

There was a very long silence from the other end of the phone. Frank braced himself for an explosion.

"I'm not even going to ask how or why you went into that apartment," Riley said quietly. "I have a forensics crew over there right now, and they'd better not find any evidence of your presence."

Frank assured him that they wouldn't and quickly hung up the phone. "I think he's pretty angry," Frank informed his brother.

"Never mind that," Joe said. "Who's dead? Peters?"

"Right," Frank replied. "Shot in the head, probably yesterday."

Joe's jaw dropped in shock. "Then he couldn't have been in the car—unless we were sideswiped by a ghost." He scowled. "But if Peters was the killer, poisoning Minkus, then setting him up to be electrocuted, who killed Peters?" He glanced at Frank. "Could he have done away with himself? You know, remorse?"

"Con Riley has ruled out suicide," Frank said, shaking his head once. "This case has more ups and downs than a roller coaster. What if Minkus was the target of three separate murder attempts that day at the mall? Peters and his poison, the Bootstompers' dud bomb, and the gimmicked microphone—"

"Which worked, except we have no idea of who set it up." Joe looked at his watch. "Mom sent me up here to bring you down for dinner. Then we have to help trim the tree."

"You go," Frank said, deep in thought. "Tell Mom I'll be there in a few minutes. First I want to print out *all* those news stories I downloaded, then I want to search some new names."

After dinner Mr. and Mrs. Hardy watched their sons attack the job of decorating the tree with almost feverish energy. "One strand at a time, please," Mrs. Hardy gently chided as Joe globbed on the tinsel. "Would anyone like more cider?" she asked on her way to the kitchen.

As soon as his mother left the room, Joe turned to Fenton. "Dad," he said, "I didn't want to startle Mom, but Hal Peters turned up murdered today."

Fenton Hardy's expression was set as his sons filled him in on the Peters situation. Mrs. Hardy walked in and saw her husband and sons deep in conversation. "You boys don't really have your heart in decorating this tree tonight, do you?" she said.

"It's pretty obvious, isn't it?" Joe said, smiling sheepishly.

His mom nodded. "We can try again tomorrow. Maybe it would help if Callie and Vanessa joined us."

"Thanks for letting us off the hook, Mom," Frank said. "Joe, let's collect those stories and get them sorted out."

"Why don't you boys give me a list of suspects, too?" Fenton suggested. "I can make some phone calls for you."

Eager for the help, Frank scribbled on a piece of paper and handed it to his father. The list read:

Dorothy Minkus
Jerry the Hammer, Dorothy's bodyguard
Hal Peters

Marian Brown
Sandy—of WAM (Women Against Minkus
or Meat)

Once they were up in Frank's room, the boys
divided the printouts into separate piles for Dorothy Minkus, Ron Minkus, Marian Brown, and
Hal Peters. "How about you take Marian and
Hal, I'll take Dorothy and Ron," Frank
suggested.

"I don't know how we're ever going to get
through all of these," Joe lamented.

Frank sat at the desk, and Joe lay on the bed,
leafing through the stacks.

"Hmmm," Joe mused. "Will you look at this?"

"What is it?"

"It seems that Hal Peters had a job in televi-
sion before joining Minkus," Joe said. "This story
says that five years ago Peters won a hundred-
thousand-dollar settlement against WFTW, when
their faulty wiring almost caused him to be
electrocuted."

Frank's eyes widened in surprise. "An interesting
coincidence, but does it make him a murderer?"

"He got the big bucks because of the pain and
suffering the electrocution caused," Joe scoffed,
"along with—get this—the electrophobia he suffered afterward."

"If that's true, there's no way Peters would
have tampered with that microphone," Frank
said.

"Come on!" Joe said. "He could've been faking. It happens all the time."

"You're right," Frank said. "Or he could have hired somebody to do the dirty work for him."

Frank raised an eyebrow and said, "He couldn't afford to pay his electric bill, but he could take out a murder contract on Minkus? I doubt it."

Joe rolled over on his back and started in on the stack of stories about Marian. After a few minutes he let out a restless groan.

"What is it, Joe?" his brother asked.

"These stories on Marian are really boring," Joe complained. "This piece goes on and on about her childhood in Maine, her collage paintings, her flatware from Spain—"

"Didn't you tell me that Marian grew up in Vermont?" Frank interrupted.

Joe frowned. "Yes, I did. Huh! Maybe the reporter got it wrong. It's all New England."

Frank read some selections on the life and times of Ron Minkus, professional bad boy. Most of the clippings were just what he expected: angry editorials, lifestyle pieces, and personality profiles.

After about half an hour Joe announced he was finished going through the stories on Marian and on Hal. "Did you find anything interesting in the Ron file?" he asked.

"Right at the bottom of the pile," Frank said.

123

"It's an ancient story about an accident Minkus had while he was in college."

"What kind of accident?"

"A car crash," Frank remarked, not looking up. "He was driving in a blizzard. The car hit a patch of ice and went out of control."

"Was he hurt?" Joe inquired.

"Sounds like it. 'Mr. Minkus is in critical condition,'" Frank read. "'His passenger, art student Jill Simpson, was pronounced dead on arrival.'"

"Wow," Joe said. "That must've been horrible for him."

"Yeah," Frank replied, shuffling through the stack. "But I don't see a mention of it in any of these other stories. Why don't we split up the Dorothy file."

Joe grabbed the top half and started reading. Within minutes his anger was building. "Dorothy sure has a great publicity staff," he said. "She's all over the papers with her All-American Agenda. When you boil it down, all she's saying is we can fix society's problems by deporting all immigrants, and we can ease racial tensions by getting rid of racial minorities."

"Here's why she wound up hospitalized," Frank said, holding up a story. "She had a breakdown in high school after being attacked by a gang. She sounds ... I'm starting to feel sorry for her here."

"You keep on reading," Joe said. "I need a

snack to keep me awake." He headed down to the kitchen, but Fenton intercepted him.

"I got something on one of your suspects."

"Dorothy?" Joe asked.

"Close," Fenton said. "Her bodyguard, Jerry, has a rap sheet a mile long, including a prison stretch for manslaughter."

"So Dorothy could have had him kill her cousin," Joe said. "Or maybe the Hammer did it on his own, thinking he was doing his boss a favor."

Still turning this new fact over in his head, Joe went into the kitchen. The phone rang, and Joe answered it. "Hello, Hardy residence," he said.

"This is Hal Peters," a croaking whisper replied in his ear. "Get off the case—or you're gonna suffer, just like Minkus did!"

Chapter

14

JOE WAS SO SURPRISED, he almost dropped the phone. "Who is this?" he yelled into the receiver. "Hello! Hello?" All he got was a dial tone.

Joe ran upstairs to tell Frank.

"Cute," Frank said. "Whoever it is figures that either we're going to be scared off or go after Peters. The person must not know Peters is dead."

Joe jammed his hands in his pockets. "Or the person doesn't know we know Peters is dead. It could be Peters's killer. I just wish I could have recognized the voice. But it was so well disguised that I couldn't even tell if it was male or female."

"What did the caller say?" Frank asked.

"Oh, the usual. Get off the case, or we'll suffer."

Frank's expression became set as he stared straight ahead. "Just a second. The voice may not be familiar," he said, "but the style rings a bell. Remember those threatening letters to Minkus? They were all into making him suffer."

"So that nut from fifteen years ago has graduated from threatening letters to phone calls?" Joe said. "But we still have no idea who it is."

The Hardys turned in right after that. Joe lay sleepless at least an hour, puzzling over the case, before he finally dropped off.

Frank shook his younger brother awake late the next morning. "Joe! We've got a press conference to go to."

"What are you talking about?" Joe asked blearily.

"It's in the newspaper." Frank cheerily waved that day's *Gazette* in his brother's face. "Dorothy Minkus is having a press conference about the supposed death threats she's been getting."

"Politics as usual," Joe muttered, dragging himself in the direction of the bathroom.

"No school this week," he complained as they trudged out to the van, "but every day I still get up at the crack of dawn."

"Since you're not a morning person," Frank said, "you'll be glad to hear I've set up an old-fashioned tree-trimming party for tonight."

Dorothy Minkus's press conference was being held in a banquet room at the Holiday House, one of Bayport's biggest hotels. Eager for more dirt on the Ron Minkus murder, the media had turned out in droves. There were news crews from as far away as Los Angeles.

Frank and Joe were able to find two seats near the front of the room. Shortly thereafter, the din fell to a murmur as Dorothy Minkus and her entourage marched to the front. The state senator was dressed in a very expensive looking, dark gray suit. To her right stood the Hammer in a black suit about a size too small. To her left was the thin reedy-faced man who had been at the funeral. He briefly scanned the audience with a sharp gaze, then stepped up to the microphone.

"Good afternoon, ladies and gentlemen. For those of you who don't know me, I am Lee Kupferberg, chief political adviser to State Senator Dorothy Minkus." His voice had the sincerity usually found in clergymen, top sales executives, and con men. "Since Dorothy's favorite cousin, Ron Minkus, died last week, requests for interviews with our senator have been overwhelming. Although she would prefer to keep her grief private"—Right, Frank thought. That's why she wanted to make a speech on Judy Minkus's porch yesterday—"Senator Minkus has decided to make a brief statement and then answer questions from the floor."

Dorothy Minkus stepped up to the microphone. First she told of receiving telephone threats in broken English. She went on to blame her cousin's death on "lawless elements" working underground like terrorists. She concluded by hinting that that sort of thing wouldn't be happening if the country had tougher immigration laws.

Frank thought her whole performance sounded exactly like that of an actress reading well-rehearsed lines for the umpteenth time. He remembered what Ron Minkus had told her— "Without the words your handlers feed into your mouth, you have nothing to say."

A reporter jumped to his feet and asked, "Is it true those were death threats you received? And when was the last one?" The senator gave a brief but dramatic statement confirming that they were death threats, the last of which had come the night before.

Another journalist asked, "Do the police agree with your theory of a foreign terrorist–type conspiracy?"

"I have spoken personally to Chief Collig of the Bayport Police Department," she answered. "Frankly, I'm disappointed with the lack of progress in their investigation of my cousin's murder."

"Can you comment on the theory that the death threats are phony, planted by someone on your staff?" someone shouted from the back.

The senator ignored the question.

Frank jumped up. "Didn't you have a rather adversarial relationship with your favorite cousin?"

Senator Minkus ignored Frank's question,

too, pointing to a well-known radio commentator from whom she could expect a friendly question.

Joe nudged his brother and pointed out Marian Brown. "I'm going to say hello to her," he said.

Frank stayed where he was and made several more attempts to ask embarrassing questions, all of which were ignored. Meanwhile, Marian looked surprised to see Joe but greeted him warmly.

"So what brings you to this baloney fest?" Joe asked with a smile.

"Oh, I wanted to keep an eye on her," Marian said. "Just make sure she doesn't smear Judy and the kids. How about you? Is Dorothy a suspect in your investigation?"

Joe shrugged noncommittally. "We thought the case was all wrapped up yesterday. But today it doesn't look so cut and dried. Did you hear about Hal Peters?"

Marian stared down at her shoes. "It was on the morning news. How terrible—he seemed a little crazy but harmless enough."

"Maybe, maybe not." Joe changed the subject. "We're researching everyone involved in the case. I've read several really nice articles about you."

"Me?" Marian said.

"We were doing background on Ron," Joe said. "Frank and I don't know too much about him. We weren't exactly regular listeners."

Marian nodded. "The show wasn't for everybody," she said. "My own mother's never heard it."

"Did the show air in Burlington?" Joe asked.

"Where?" Marian said.

"Isn't that where your mom lives?"

"Vermont?" Marian shook her head. "Oh, no. She lives in Maine."

Joe looked perplexed. "I thought you told me you were going back home to Burlington."

"Must have been a slip of the tongue," she said. "I lived in Vermont for a while when I was a little kid. Guess I was thinking back to younger and happier days. My family is in Maine." She glanced at her watch. "Got to run. Nice seeing you, Joe."

The press conference was breaking up. Joe found his brother facing Jerry the Hammer, who seemed to be looking for a rematch. Joe dashed over, but Con Riley got there first and stepped between the two.

"Take a hike, you goon," the police officer growled at the bodyguard. The big man skulked off.

Joe told Riley about the mystery phone call and, after the officer left, filled his brother in on his chat with Marian.

"Strange," Frank said. "She tells the newspaper one thing and tells you another."

"Well, this time she went back to what the newspaper said," Joe pointed out.

"I don't buy this slip-of-the-tongue excuse," Frank said. "It's more like she's covering something up. Maybe she knew Minkus in Burlington and doesn't want anyone to know about it."

Joe nodded. "Suppose they were romantically involved a long time ago," he suggested.

"Good thinking, Joe," Frank said. "Marian wouldn't want Judy or the kids to know."

"Why don't we pay Marian a visit and find out for sure?" Joe suggested.

The Hardys made the trip from the hotel to Marian Brown's place in just under fifteen minutes. They had no trouble finding the house because Sarah had pointed it out when they had driven her home from Mr. Pizza.

Marian answered the door on the second knock. She seemed a little flustered. "Oh, hi. What are you two doing here?"

"Joe told me he saw you at Dorothy's press conference," Frank said with a friendly smile. "I just wanted to ask you a few questions about her. Do you mind if we come in for a few minutes?"

Marian relaxed and motioned them inside. "Grab a box and sit down," she said. "The movers already took the sofa. Can I get you a soda?"

When Marian returned with soft drinks, Frank asked her how long she had known Dorothy Minkus. Marian thought a moment before she answered. "Probably as long as I've known Ron."

"Were they always at each other's throats?" Joe asked.

Marian's eyes grew large. "You don't think—"

"We *think* a lot," Frank said. "We don't *know* much—"

"Well, they always disagreed politically," Marian said. "But the real feud didn't begin until that fight on the show. I suppose you know about it. She lost her first election. But she won the next one. Her staff ran the campaign on how the media had smeared her. After that, the show got nastier. Ron wasn't happy about it, but that's what brought in the ratings. He became the world's favorite equal-opportunity offender."

"So both Ron and Dorothy wound up playing roles and getting famous," Frank said.

"I suppose that's a good way of putting it," Marian said.

Joe decided to change the subject. "I read about your art collection. Is it all packed?"

"Yes," she said. "My lovely paintings are on a slow van to New England even as we speak."

"What do you collect?" Frank asked.

"A little-known artist from New England. She used paint and collage techniques in a unique style. I've tried to copy it, but it's hard. Her paintings were almost ... magical. You'd always find something new in them." Marian's eyes seemed almost misty as she spoke. Then she came back to earth. "Are you boys art lovers?"

"Not really," Frank said, a bit embarrassed,

133

"unless you count football as an art form. Would you mind if I asked you something personal?"

"That would depend on the question."

"Please don't be offended," Frank began. "But were you and Ron ever ... ever ..."

"Romantically involved?" Marian finished the question. Frank and Joe nodded.

Marian laughed. "Ron was like a brother to me," she said. "The police already asked me that question. How ridiculous!"

"I was just curious because of the Burlington connection," Joe tried to explain. "You mentioned you lived there, and that's where Ron went to college. I thought maybe you'd gotten together there and you didn't want Judy Minkus to find out."

Marian smiled. "You boys must have very rich fantasy lives. I was just a kid in Burlington, too young to date. Ron and I met working at a station in Cleveland. Sorry, guys. Now if you'll excuse me, I have packing to finish."

As Marian walked them to the door, Frank picked up a photograph. "Is this your family?" he asked.

Marian nodded, her eyes growing misty again.

Joe looked over his brother's shoulder. The photo showed two slim teenage girls with their parents. Neither had any resemblance to Marian. "Why aren't you in it?" he asked.

"Someone had to snap the picture—me," Marian said, opening the door. "Sorry I couldn't help you any more. Goodbye."

Frank noticed Marian watching from the living room window as they walked back to the van. "She's hiding something," he said. "I think we have to take a harder look at Marian Brown."

Joe nodded. "Why don't we stop by the Minkus place and see what Sarah has to say about her?"

The lawn in front of the Minkus house was refreshingly clear of reporters when the Hardys drove up. Mrs. Minkus answered the door and welcomed the two warmly. "Sarah, your detective friends are here," she called up the stairs.

Sarah looked happy but surprised to see Frank and Joe. "I apologize for not calling first," Frank said, "but we were in the area and we just wanted to see how you were doing."

As they walked into the family room, Frank noticed a painting on the far wall. It was part collage and partly drawn, just like the ones Marian described in her collection.

"I never noticed that before," Frank commented.

"Isn't it gorgeous?" Sarah said with a smile. "Marian did it."

"Really?" Joe said. "I guess you're going to miss her a lot when she moves."

Sarah nodded sadly. "I don't know what we would have done without her these last few days.

She was such a comfort. My dad always trusted her. He said she felt like an old friend from the day he met her."

Frank stood in front of the painting, studying it carefully. The phone rang, and Sarah ran from the room to answer it. Suddenly Frank turned to his brother.

"Look at this," he whispered urgently, pointing at the painting.

With the many pasted-on, painted-over letters and photographs that made up the painting, it took Joe awhile to pick out what Frank saw.

Slowly he focused on a slash of red paint that zigzagged across the canvas. It was like a path connecting certain letters. And those letters formed a message: H-E-K-I-L-L-J-I-L-L!

Chapter

15

"JILL ... JILL ..." Frank said, searching for a connection. Where had that name come up?

Then he remembered. "That old newspaper story about Minkus's accident. The girl who died was an art student—"

"Named Jill," Joe said. "And here's Marian Brown copying the style of an unknown artist from New England. Maybe that artist is from Burlington, Vermont."

"The threatening notes," Frank suddenly said. "The oldest was mailed to Ron Minkus in Burlington."

"They were done in pasted-on letters," Joe said, following Frank's logic. "That's a form of collage. Even Tori knew that!"

Sarah returned to the room. "That's so weird,"

she said. "Here we were admiring that painting, and Marian calls, asking if she can have it back. She said since she painted it for my dad, it would remind her of him. Isn't that sweet?"

"Wonderful," Frank said through tight lips.

Sarah sensed the sudden tension in the room. "Are you guys okay?"

"Fine," Joe assured her.

"But late," Frank quickly added, tapping his watch. "I just realized we were supposed to be home almost an hour ago."

Sarah looked disappointed that they were leaving so quickly. "Well, come back and visit soon," she said.

"Count on it," Frank said as he and Joe rushed to the door. They jumped back in their van and burned rubber back to Marian's house.

"We've got to figure out how to lead up to this. See if you can find that article about Minkus's car crash, Joe," Frank said, pointing to the file folder on the floor of the van.

Joe grabbed the folder and flipped through it. "Here," he said as Frank pulled into Marian's driveway. "The victim was an art student named Jill Simpson." Joe quickly read. "She was survived by her mother, Phyllis; her father, Joseph; and her sister, Mary Ann."

"Mary Ann ... Marian," Frank said, pulling into the driveway and throwing the van into Park. "Let me see that."

Frank leaned over to take the story from

his brother's hand. But he never got a chance to read it because he was interrupted by the sight of a .38 revolver pointing directly at Joe's head.

"Open up!" Marian Brown barked through the window. She stepped away so the swinging door wouldn't block her and resumed a two-handed firing stance. "You"—she nodded at Joe—"in the back."

Marian jumped into the passenger seat as Joe moved to the rear of the vehicle. Cocking her gun and pointing it at Frank, she growled, "Drive."

Frank pulled out of the driveway and followed her directions to a seedy section of Bayport. In the distance Frank could see a deserted industrial park.

After a couple of minutes of tense silence, Frank glanced over at Marian. "Don't look at me, just drive," she snapped, pushing the gun into his temple.

"We saw the painting, Marian," Frank said, keeping his eyes forward. "You were right, an artist *can* reveal a lot through her work."

"Shut up!" she said.

"Who was Jill Simpson to you?" Joe asked from the rear, hoping to distract her.

"None of your business." Marian's voice was tough, but Frank could feel the gun trembling against his head.

"You know, Ron Minkus wasn't responsible

for her death," Frank said. Joe was amazed at how calm his brother's voice sounded.

"How would you know?" she screamed. "How would you know anything!" Marian took a deep breath. "All you know is Ron Minkus—devoted husband and father." She spat the words out. "That's nothing but a lie. He's a killer. He donated all that money to charity and adopted those girls to try to atone for the *murder* he committed!"

Her voice caught in her throat, and she began to sob. Joe calmly asked again, "Marian, who was Jill Simpson?"

"Jill Simpson was my beautiful, talented older sister," Marian said through her tears.

"Was she in that picture I saw at your house?" he asked softly.

"We both were." Marian's voice grew hard again. "I was afraid Minkus would recognize me—we looked too much alike. So I put on weight, changed my hair color, had it permed—"

Frank gave her a sidelong glance. The girls in the picture had been slim and pretty. Marian—Mary Ann Simpson—had completely changed her appearance to pursue vengeance.

"Did you kill Hal Peters?" Joe asked.

"Of course," Marian said. "Too bad you didn't think of that before." Her tears had stopped, and she burst out in a rage again. "You were fools and so was he! That idiot couldn't do anything right!"

Frank caught his brother's eye in the rearview mirror. "I understand he was fired for that very reason," he said.

"Who cares about the show?" Marian snapped. "He was supposed to kill Ron. I paid him good money to do it. Peters became a health freak after his accident. He said he knew a way to make a person suffer a long, drawn-out death. But *noooo,* he never got the right amount of arsenic. He just made Ron Minkus throw up a lot! And then he got himself fired!"

The car was getting very close to the derelict factory area. "But he did finally kill Ron, didn't he, Marian?" Frank asked.

"That wimp just didn't have the stomach for it," she said in disgust. "*I* had to rig the mike. Believe me, that was no easy task. Then, after I succeeded, Hal thought he could blackmail me. He was having money troubles; he threatened to go to the police if I didn't pay him off."

Marian grimaced. "But he screwed up, as usual. I made sure he'll never do that again."

Frank heard his brother take a deep breath. "So you've killed two people because your sister died in an accident," Joe said.

"My sister was killed by Ron Minkus!" Marian shrieked. "Ron Minkus was a murderer, so Ron Minkus had to die. The Bible says so. An eye for an eye. I killed two guys, and now I'm going to kill two more."

Frank saw that even though the gun was still aimed at him, Marian had turned in her seat to shout at Joe. The street ahead of them was deserted. It dead-ended at the entrance to the abandoned industrial park. A rusty chain-link fence hung drunkenly off one hinge. The van was barely crawling forward. Frozen snow and ice rutted the road, which apparently hadn't seen a snowplow.

Now was the time. Frank gunned the engine. The van swerved and bounced on the slippery surface. For an instant the madwoman and her gun were knocked off balance.

"What are you doing?" she screamed as Joe launched himself over the seat at her. He grabbed Marian's gun hand and struggled to push her up against the dashboard.

Marian snarled and pushed her free hand into Joe's face, her nails clawing deep into his skin.

Frank couldn't help. He was desperately trying to control their wild skid. The van nearly rammed a derelict tractor-trailer.

Marian fought like a woman possessed, and Joe was in an awkward position, stretched out across the seat back. The van lurched and bumped again. Joe lost his grip on Marian's wrist. She smashed the gun into the side of his head, and Joe sank behind the seat.

Frank finally got control of the van when it was right beside the rusty fence. But Marian was swinging the gun in line with Frank's head again. Frank hit the gas pedal and the van leaped forward. Marian's arm bounced, but her finger tightened on the trigger.

Frank threw up a hand, and the deafening *boom!* of a gunshot rang out.

Chapter

16

FRANK'S HAND hit Marian's wrist just as the van hit the fence. The shock of the impact had moved the gun just enough for the shot to miss Frank and blow out the windshield instead.

Frank let go of the wheel, grappling for the gun. Suddenly Joe appeared from behind the seat, seizing Marian in a choke hold.

Together, they managed to subdue her as the van slid to a stop. "You okay, Frank?" Joe yelled, unable to see his brother because of Marian's flailing.

"I'm fine," Frank assured him as he wrenched the gun away from her grip. "No problems that Bayport Auto Glass won't be able to fix."

A police cruiser skidded to a halt behind them.

Not wanting to spook the officers approaching from either side, guns drawn, Frank leaned out, showing empty hands.

"Radio Con Riley!" he yelled. "My name is Frank Hardy. Tell him we've apprehended Ron Minkus's murderer!"

The officers came over to the van, pulled open the doors, handcuffed Marian, and put her in the back of the police car.

Soon another squad car came lurching up, siren blaring. Con Riley got out. The officers must have radioed him. He walked directly over to the Hardys. "Are you sure she's the murderer?"

"She admitted it," Frank assured him, "when she thought she was about to blow us away." He handed the gun to Riley. "And that should be the murder weapon for Hal Peters."

"But why?" the officer asked. "We couldn't find any kind of record on her."

"That's because Marian Brown doesn't exist. Her real name is Mary Ann Simpson," Frank explained. "Her sister, Jill, died in a car accident years ago. Guess who was driving."

"Ron Minkus," Riley said. "I got the accident report as part of his file. What about Peters?"

"He was poisoning Minkus," Joe said. "She hired him. He tried to blackmail her, so she killed him."

"We'll have to take complete statements down at the station," Riley told them. The officer glanced at the spot where their windshield had been. "Do you guys need a ride?"

"No, thanks," Frank answered. "A little fresh air never hurt anyone." He took the snow brush from underneath the driver's seat and swept the glass off the dashboard.

As they drove slowly toward the police station, the cold wind blasting their faces, Joe turned to his brother and said, "I sure don't want to be the one to tell the Minkuses that Marian is the killer."

Frank gave him a grim nod. "Lucky for us, that's a police job."

When they finally reached the station, a young officer took their statements, and then they were joined by Con Riley.

"We've just about finished our interrogation of Marian Brown," Riley said. "If you want to call it that. She confessed to both murders on the ride over. After fifteen years of holding it in, she's letting the whole story gush out."

Riley shook his head and continued. "She's been stalking Minkus for years. He met her once, before the accident, and that's why she changed her appearance so much. She even got a nose job."

"How did she end up working with him?" Joe wondered.

"She's a very smart woman," Riley said. "She learned the radio business inside and out, then went to work at a station where he was a DJ.

When she heard he was hiring a sidekick, she applied and got the job."

"I wonder why she kept writing those threatening letters," Joe asked.

"How did you know she did that?" Riley asked.

"Gee, Officer, don't you know anything about art?" Joe asked. "Marian used the same technique of collage in the letters as she did in her paintings. Why, a six-year-old could've figured that out," he said, recalling little Tori's earlier remark.

"Quit showing off, Joe," Frank said. "We figured it from the time and place of the first letter—Burlington, not long after the accident."

"She tried to ruin his life," Riley said. "She didn't start off planning to kill him; she just wanted him to suffer."

"It must have really bothered her to see him so happy and successful," Frank said.

"Exactly," Riley said. "Just before his death, Minkus signed a big-bucks syndication deal. It was going to make both him and Marian rich beyond their wildest dreams. It also pushed her over the edge. She got Peters to start poisoning him during the negotiations. When Peters got fired, she took over, dosing Minkus's coffee at work. But when he signed, she decided to end it once and for all. She confessed to everything."

"Weird," Joe said. "The people he attacked on

the air had nothing to do with his death. He was killed by someone he thought was a friend."

"Bobby Hadrava might have killed him," Riley pointed out, "if that bomb had worked. Personally, I'm glad we're able to put Hadrava away. As for that woman with the flowers—that was just a very sick young lady's idea of a political statement."

"I guess that wraps it up," Joe said, "except for the ghost car that chased us."

"That had to be Marian," Frank said. "After she killed Peters, she used his car, then she called us and disguised her voice."

"In the end, you two helped us track down a very clever criminal," Riley said, and offered the Hardys his hand. "Thanks, guys."

After shaking hands with both of them, Riley headed for the exit. "I'm going over to the Minkus house to take the painting into evidence," he said. "They already know about Marian. I told them over the phone. Would you like a ride?"

This time they accepted Riley's offer, figuring they'd have no problem begging a ride home from their mom since their tree-trimming was planned for later.

Judy Minkus was red eyed and puffy faced from crying when she opened the door. She greeted Frank and Joe with a grateful hug, still crying a little. "I can't believe it was Marian.

Of all people, I really thought she was our friend."

"We're so sorry," Joe said.

Officer Riley apologized for the interruption, picked up the painting, and returned to work in his squad car. Frank and Joe joined the rest of the family in the living room.

The doorbell chimed, and Sarah jumped up from the couch with a smile on her face. "That would be Chet," she said.

"Chet!" they heard Sarah exclaim from the front hall. "You guys didn't have to do that!"

Chet marched into the room, a bright red cap with a white pom-pom covering his shaved head. He was followed by Callie and Vanessa, who were helping him carry a big Christmas tree. Tori jumped up from the couch and clapped her hands. "Santa's here!" she yelped excitedly.

Mrs. Minkus beamed. "You kids are so thoughtful," she said. "Thank you so much."

Chet blushed. "I know Tori's a big fan of the man in red."

The doorbell rang again, and Judy Minkus went to answer it. She came back, followed by Dorothy Minkus, who was carrying two bags of gifts. The Hammer was nowhere in sight.

"Look who's here, kids," Mrs. Minkus announced with a hopeful smile. "It's Cousin Dorothy."

Sarah and Tori stood still arm and arm and looked at their cousin curiously.

Dorothy put down the bags and stretched her

hands to Judy. "I wanted you all to be the first to know. I'm retiring from politics. Years ago Ron accused me of being a phony. His words came back to haunt me today, after the press conference. My cousin was murdered, and what did I do about it? I stood in front of a microphone and just repeated what Lee Kupferberg and his staff told me to say. Ron was right."

She faced the girls, trying to force her mouth into a smile. "I know I haven't been the nicest person in the world." Dorothy's usually cool voice cracked. "But I'd like to make up for that—with these presents, for a start."

Tori's eyes lit up. "Presents? For me?"

Dorothy nodded, her smile getting brighter.

Sarah still looked doubtful. "For you, too, Sarah," Dorothy said.

"I really don't want your presents," Sarah said stiffly.

"Sarah, try to understand," Dorothy said. "I was playing a part, not a very nice part."

"Like 'Radio Ron,'" Judy said.

"Ron and I had our differences," Dorothy admitted. "But we were family, and so are you. Believe it or not, deep down I love you, and I also loved your father."

"That's the first time I ever heard you say that," Sarah said softly.

Frank poked Joe. "I think we're getting in the way of a family celebration," he whispered.

Frank, Joe, Callie, Vanessa, and Chet said their goodbyes, promising to visit soon.

As they stepped outside, they saw it had started snowing again.

"Well," Frank said, a little smile gradually coming to his lips. "It's finally beginning to look a lot like Christmas."

Frank and Joe's next case:

Frank and Joe's friend Davis Johns is one of the hottest high school basketball prospects in the state, and two colleges are going all out to sign him. But the competition between the two programs is getting downright ugly. And now the game has taken an even more sinister turn: The head coach at Bayport U. has suddenly dropped dead! The Hardys are convinced that the death is a result of foul play, and they're determined to slam-dunk the case. But the killer is running the show, he's still got a few shots left, and he's aiming them right at Frank and Joe. The boys know that the clock is ticking down and that losing this game could be murder... in *Fast Break*, Case #107 in The Hardy Boys Casefiles™.

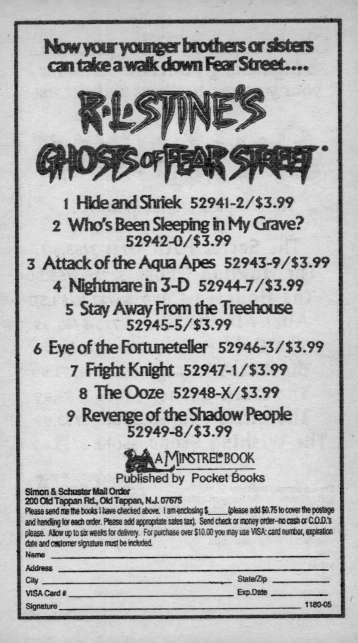

THE HARDY BOYS CASEFILES

☐ #1: DEAD ON TARGET	73992-1/$3.99		☐ #75: NO WAY OUT	73111-4/$3.99
☐ #2: EVIL, INC.	73668-X/$3.75		☐ #76: TAGGED FOR TERROR	73112-2/$3.99
☐ #3: CULT OF CRIME	68726-3/$3.99		☐ #77: SURVIVAL RUN	79461-2/$3.99
☐ #4: THE LAZARUS PLOT	73995-6/$3.75		☐ #78: THE PACIFIC CONSPIRACY	79462-0/$3.99
☐ #5: EDGE OF DESTRUCTION	73669-8/$3.99		☐ #79: DANGER UNLIMITED	79463-9/$3.99
☐ #6: THE CROWNING OF TERROR	73670-1/$3.50		☐ #80: DEAD OF NIGHT	79464-7/$3.99
☐ #7: DEATHGAME	73672-8/$3.99		☐ #81: SHEER TERROR	79465-5/$3.99
☐ #8: SEE NO EVIL	73673-6/$3.50		☐ #82: POISONED PARADISE	79466-3/$3.99
☐ #9: THE GENIUS THIEVES	73674-4/$3.50		☐ #83: TOXIC REVENGE	79467-1/$3.99
☐ #12: PERFECT GETAWAY	73675-2/$3.50		☐ #84: FALSE ALARM	79468-X/$3.99
☐ #14: TOO MANY TRAITORS	73677-9/$3.50		☐ #85: WINNER TAKE ALL	79469-8/$3.99
☐ #32: BLOOD MONEY	74665-0/$3.50		☐ #86: VIRTUAL VILLAINY	79470-1/$3.99
☐ #35: THE DEAD SEASON	74105-5/$3.50		☐ #87: DEAD MAN IN DEADWOOD	79471-X/$3.99
☐ #41: HIGHWAY ROBBERY	70038-3/$3.75		☐ #88: INFERNO OF FEAR	79472-8/$3.99
☐ #44: CASTLE FEAR	74615-4/$3.75		☐ #89: DARKNESS FALLS	79473-6/$3.99
☐ #45: IN SELF-DEFENSE	70042-1/$3.75		☐ #90: DEADLY ENGAGEMENT	79474-4/$3.99
☐ #47: FLIGHT INTO DANGER	70044-8/$3.99		☐ #91: HOT WHEELS	79475-2/$3.99
☐ #49: DIRTY DEEDS	70046-4/$3.99		☐ #92: SABOTAGE AT SEA	79476-0/$3.99
☐ #50: POWER PLAY	70047-2/$3.99		☐ #93: MISSION: MAYHEM	88204-X/$3.99
☐ #53: WEB OF HORROR	73089-4/$3.99		☐ #94: A TASTE FOR TERROR	88205-8/$3.99
☐ #54: DEEP TROUBLE	73090-8/$3.99		☐ #95: ILLEGAL PROCEDURE	88206-6/$3.99
☐ #55: BEYOND THE LAW	73091-6/$3.50		☐ #96: AGAINST ALL ODDS	88207-4/$3.99
☐ #56: HEIGHT OF DANGER	73092-4/$3.99		☐ #97: PURE EVIL	88208-2/$3.99
☐ #57: TERROR ON TRACK	73093-2/$3.99		☐ #98: MURDER BY MAGIC	88209-0/$3.99
☐ #60: DEADFALL	73096-7/$3.75		☐ #99: FRAME-UP	88210-4/$3.99
☐ #61: GRAVE DANGER	73097-5/$3.99		☐ #100: TRUE THRILLER	88211-2/$3.99
☐ #62: FINAL GAMBIT	73098-3/$3.75		☐ #101: PEAK OF DANGER	88212-0/$3.99
☐ #64: ENDANGERED SPECIES	73100-9/$3.99		☐ #102: WRONG SIDE OF THE LAW	88213-9/$3.99
☐ #65: NO MERCY	73101-7/$3.99		☐ #103: CAMPAIGN OF CRIME	88214-7/$3.99
☐ #66: THE PHOENIX EQUATION	73102-5/$3.99		☐ #104: WILD WHEELS	88215-5/$3.99
☐ #68: ROUGH RIDING	73104-1/$3.75		☐ #105: LAW OF THE JUNGLE	50426-2/$3.99
☐ #69: MAYHEM IN MOTION	73105-X/$3.75		☐ #106: SHOCK JOCK	50429-0/$3.99
☐ #71: REAL HORROR	73107-6/$3.99		☐ #107: FAST BREAK	50430-4/$3.99
☐ #72: SCREAMERS	73108-4/$3.75		☐ #108: BLOWN AWAY	50431-2/$3.99
☐ #73: BAD RAP	73109-2/$3.99		☐ #109: MOMENT OF TRUTH	50432-0/$3.99
☐ #74: ROAD PIRATES	73110-6/$3.99		☐ #110: BAD CHEMISTRY	50433-9/$3.99